Allan Quatermain

Also available by H. Rider Haggard

KING SOLOMON'S MINES

ALLAN QUATERMAIN

Ex Africa semper aliquid novi

H. Rider Haggard

Abridged by Sarah Litvinoff

Beaver Books

I INSCRIBE THIS BOOK OF ADVENTURE
TO MY SON
ARTHUR JOHN RIDER HAGGARD
IN THE HOPE THAT IN DAYS TO COME HE,
AND MANY OTHER BOYS WHOM I SHALL NEVER KNOW,
MAY,
IN THE ACTS AND THOUGHTS OF ALLAN QUATERMAIN
AND HIS COMPANIONS, AS HEREIN RECORDED,
FIND SOMETHING TO HELP HIM AND THEM TO REACH
TO WHAT, WITH SIR HENRY CURTIS, I HOLD TO BE THE
HIGHEST RANK WHERETO WE CAN ATTAIN—
THE STATE AND DIGNITY OF ENGLISH GENTLEMEN

A Beaver Book
Published by Arrow Books Limited
62–5 Chandos Place, London WC2N 4NW

An imprint of Century Hutchinson Ltd

London Melbourne Sydney Auckland
Johannesburg and agencies throughout the world

First published 1887
Beaver edition 1986

Set in Linotron Plantin by
Rowland Phototypesetting Limited
Bury St Edmunds, Suffolk
Made and printed in Great Britain
by Anchor Brendon Limited
Tiptree, Essex

ISBN 0 09 945550 1

ONE
The Consul's Yarn

A week had passed since the funeral of my only son. Poor Harry to go so soon! Carried off by the very smallpox virus he had hoped to cure. We buried him on a dreary December afternoon, and the sky was heavy with snow. The coffin was put down by the grave and a few big flakes lit upon it. They looked very white upon the black cloth. A robin redbreast came as bold as could be and lit upon the coffin and began to sing. And then I am afraid that I broke down, and so did Sir Henry Curtis, strong man though he is; and as for Captain Good, I saw him turn away too; even in my own distress I could not help noticing it.

One evening a week later, I was in my room walking up and down and thinking. I was now all alone in the world, and I realized that I longed for the wild land of Africa where I had spent my life. No man who has for forty years lived the life of an explorer can go coop himself in the prim English country, with its trim hedgerows and cultivated fields, its stiff formal manner and its well-dressed crowds. He begins to long – ah how he longs! – for the keen breath of the desert air, and his heart rises up in rebellion against the strict limits of the cultivated life.

As I was musing there was a ring at the outer door. Going down the steps I opened it myself, and in came my old friends Sir Henry Curtis and Captain John Good, RN. They entered the vestibule and sat themselves down before the wide hearth, where, I remember, a particularly good fire of logs was burning.

'It is very kind of you to come round,' I said by way of making a remark; 'it must have been heavy walking in the snow.'

They said nothing, but Sir Henry slowly filled his pipe and lit it with a burning ember. As he leant forward to do so the fire got hold of a grassy bit of pine and flared up brightly, throwing the whole scene into strong relief, and I thought, what a splendid-looking man he is! Calm, powerful face, clear-cut features, large grey eyes, yellow beard and hair – altogether a magnificent specimen.

Nor did his form belie his face. I have never seen wider shoulders or a deeper chest. Indeed, Sir Henry's girth is so great that, though he is six feet two high, he does not strike one as a tall man. As I looked at him I could not help thinking what a curious contrast my little dried-up self presented to his grand face and form.

I, Allan Quatermain, commonly called Hunter Quatermain, or by the natives 'Macumazahn' – he who keeps a bright look-out at night, or, in vulgar English, a sharp fellow who is not to be taken in.

Then there was Good, who is not like either of us, being short, dark, stout – *very* stout – with twinkling black eyes, in one of which an eyeglass is everlastingly fixed. I say stout, but it is a mild term; I regret to state that of late years Good has been running to fat in a most disgraceful way. Sir Henry tells him that it comes from idleness and over-feeding, and Good does not like it at all, though he cannot deny it.

They sat and smoked and drank whisky and water, and I stood by the fire also smoking and looking at them.

At last I spoke. 'Old friends,' I said, 'how long is it since we got back from Kukuanaland?'

'Three years,' said Good. 'Why do you ask?'

'I ask because I think that I have had a long enough spell of civilization. I am going back to the veldt.'

Sir Henry laid his head back in his arm-chair and laughed one of his deep laughs. 'How very odd,' he said, 'while we were walking here we were talking about a little plan that I have formed – namely, that if you were willing we should pack up our traps and go off to Africa on another expedition.'

I fairly jumped at his words. 'You don't say so!' I said.

'Yes I do, though, and so does Good; don't you, Good?'

'Rather,' said that gentleman.

'Listen, old fellow,' went on Sir Henry, with considerable animation of manner. 'I'm tired of it too, dead-tired of doing nothing except play the squire in a country that is sick of squires. For a year or more I have been getting as restless as an old elephant who scents danger. I am always dreaming of Kukuanaland and Gagool and King Solomon's Mines. I can assure you I have become the victim of an almost unaccountable craving. I am sick of shooting pheasants and partridges, and want to have a go at some large game again.'

'Ah!' I said, 'And Good, what is your reason for wanting to trek; have you got one?'

'I have,' said Good, solemnly. 'I never do anything without a reason if you really want to know, though I'd rather not speak of a delicate and strictly personal matter, I'll tell you: I'm getting too fat.'

'Shut up, Good!' said Sir Henry. 'And now, Quatermain, tell us, where do you propose going to?'

I lit my pipe, which had gone out, before answering.

'Have you people ever heard of Mt Kenia?' I asked.

'Don't know the place,' said Good.

'Did you ever hear of the Island of Lamu?' I asked again.

'No. Stop, though – isn't it a place about 300 miles north of Zanzibar?'

'Yes. Now listen. What I have to propose is this. That we go to Lamu and thence make our way about 250 miles inland to Mt Kenia; from Mt Kenia on inland to Mt Lekakisera, another 200 miles, or thereabouts, beyond which no white man has to the best of my belief ever been; and then, if we get so far, right on into the unknown interior. What do you say to that, my hearties?'

'It's a big order,' said Sir Henry, reflectively.

'You are right,' I answered, 'it is; but I take it that we are all three of us in search of a big order. We want a change of scene, and we are likely to get one – a thorough change. All my life I have longed to visit those parts, and I mean to do it before I die. My poor boy's death has broken the last link between me and civilization, and I'm off to my native wilds. And now I'll tell you another thing, and that is, that for years and years I have heard rumours of a great white race which is supposed to have its home somewhere up in this direction, and I have a mind to see if there is any truth in them. If you fellows like to come, well and good; if not, I'll go alone.'

'I'm your man, though I don't believe in your white race,' said Sir Henry Curtis, rising and placing his arm upon my shoulder.

'Ditto,' remarked Good; 'I'll go into training at once. By all means let's go to Mt Kenia and the other place with an unpronounceable name, and look for a white race that does not exist. It's all one to me.'

'When do you propose to start?' asked Sir Henry.

'This day month,' I answered, 'by the British India steamboat; and don't you be so certain that things have no existence because you do not happen to have heard of them. Remember King Solomon's Mines!'

Some fourteen weeks or so had passed since the date of this conversation, and this history goes on its way in very different surroundings.

It came to pass that on arriving at the island of Lamu, we disembarked with all our goods and chattels, and, not knowing where to go, marched boldly up to the house of Her Majesty's Consul, where we were most hospitably received.

'Well, where are you gentlemen steering for?' asked the Consul, as we smoked our pipes after dinner.

'We propose to go to Mt Kenia and then on to Mt Lekakisera,' answered Sir Henry. 'Quatermain has got hold of some yarn about there being a white race up in the unknown territories beyond.'

The Consul looked interested, and answered that he had heard something of that, too.

'What have you heard?' I asked.

'Oh, not much. All I know about it is that a year or so ago I got a letter from Mackenzie, the Scotch missionary, whose station, "The Highlands", is placed at the highest navigable point of the Tana River, in which he said something about it.'

'Have you the letter?' I asked.

'No, I destroyed it; but I remember that he said that a man had arrived at his station who declared that two months' journey beyond Mt Lekakisera, which no white man has yet visited – at least, so far as I know – he found a lake called Laga, and that then he went off to the north-east, a month's journey, over desert and thorn veldt and great mountains, till he came to a country where the people are white and live in stone houses. Here he was hospitably entertained for a while, till at last the priests of the country set it about that he was a devil, and the people drove him away, and he journeyed for eight months and reached Mackenzie's place, as I heard, dying. That's all I know; and if you ask me, I believe that it is a lie; but if you want to find out more about it, you had better go up the Tana to Mackenzie's place and ask him for information.'

Sir Henry and I looked at each other. Here was something tangible.

'I think that we will go to Mr Mackenzie's,' I said.

'Well,' answered the Consul, 'that is your best way, but I warn you that you are likely to have a rough journey, for I hear that the Masai are about, and, as you know, they are not pleasant customers.'

Fortunately there were at Lamu at this time a party of Wakwafi Askari (soldiers). The Wakwafi, who are a cross between the Masai and the Wataveta, are a fine manly race. They are also great hunters. As it happened, these particular men had recently been on a long trip with an Englishman named Jutson, who had died of fever when on his return journey. His hunters buried him, and then came on to Lamu in a dhow. Our friend the Consul suggested to us that we had better try and hire these men, and accordingly on the following morning we started to interview the party, accompanied by an interpreter.

In due course we found them in a mud hut on the outskirts of the town. Three of the men were sitting outside the hut, and fine frank-looking fellows they were. To them we cautiously opened the object of our visit, at first with very scant success. They declared that they could not entertain any such idea, that they were worn and weary with long travelling, and that their hearts were sore at the loss of their master. They meant to go back to their homes and rest awhile. This did not sound very promising, so by way of effecting a diversion I asked where the remainder of them were. I was told there were six, and I saw but three. One of the men said that they slept in the hut, and were yet resting after their labours.

Presently they came out of the hut, yawning – the first two men being evidently of the same race and style as those already before us; but the appearance of the third and last nearly made me jump out of my skin. He was a very tall, broad man, quite six foot three, I should say, but gaunt, with lean, wiry-looking limbs. My first glance at him told me that he was no Wakwafi: he was a pure bred Zulu. He came out with his thin aristocratic-looking hand placed before his face to hide a yawn, so I could only see that he had a great three-cornered hole in his forehead. In another second he removed his hand, revealing a powerful-looking Zulu face, with a humorous mouth, a short woolly beard, tinged with grey, and a pair of brown eyes keen as a hawk's. I knew my man at once, although I had not seen him for twelve years. 'How do you do, Umslopogaas?' I said quietly in Zulu.

The tall man started, and almost let the long-handled battle-axe he held in his hand fall in his astonishment. Next second he had recognized me, and was saluting me in an outburst of sonorous language which made his companions the Wakwafi stare.

'Koos' (chief), he began, 'Koos-y-Pagate! Koos-y-umcool! (Chief from of old – mighty chief) Koos! Baba! (father) Macumazahn, old hunter, slayer of elephants, eater up of lions, clever one! watchful one! brave one! quick one! whose shot never misses, who strikes straight home, who grasps a hand and holds it to the death (i.e. is a true friend). Behold! a messenger came up from Natal, "Macumazahn is dead!" cried he. "The land knows Macumazahn no more." That is years ago. And now, behold, now in this strange place I find Macumazahn, my friend. The brush of the old jackal has gone a little grey; but is not his eye as keen, and are not his teeth as sharp?'

I had let him run on thus because I saw that his enthusiasm was producing a marked effect upon the minds of the five Wakwafi, who appeared to understand something of his talk; but now I thought it time to put a stop to it.

'Silence!' I said. 'Has all thy noisy talk been stopped up since last I saw thee that it breaks out thus, and sweeps us away? What doest thou here with these men – thou whom I left a chief in Zululand? How is it that thou art far from thine own place, and gathered together with strangers?'

Umslopogaas leant himself upon the head of his long battle-axe (which was nothing else but a pole-axe, with a beautiful handle of rhinoceros horn), and his grim face grew sad.

'My Father,' he answered, 'I have a word to tell thee, but I cannot speak it before these people. It is for thine own ear. My Father, this will I say,' and here his face grew stern again, 'a woman betrayed me to the death, and covered my name with shame – my own wife, a round-faced girl, betrayed me; but I escaped from death; I broke from the very hands of those who came to slay me. I struck but three blows with this mine axe Inkosi-kaas – surely my Father will remember it – one to the right, one to the left, and one in front, and yet I left three men dead. And then I fled, and, as my Father knows, even now that I am old there breathes not the man who, by running, can touch me again when once I have bounded from his side. Then I fled north. Nought have I brought save this mine axe; of all my belongings this remains alone. They have divided my cattle; they have taken my wives; and my children know my face no more. Yet with this axe' – and he swung the formidable weapon round his head, making the air hiss as he clove it – 'will I cut another path to fortune. I have spoken.'

I shook my head at him, 'Behold, Umslopogaas, I know thee for a great warrior and a brave man, faithful to the death. Hear me now. We three whom thou seest, Incubu,' and I pointed to Curtis, 'Bougwan,' and I pointed to Good, 'and myself would travel inland far into the unknown beyond. We go to hunt and seek adventures, and new places. Wilt thou come with us? To thee shall be given command of all our servants; but what shall befall thee, that I know not. Mayhap death awaits thee and us. Wilt thou throw thyself to Fortune and come, or fearest thou, Umslopogaas?'

The great man smiled. 'So we are going to see something like the old times again, Macumazahn, when we fought and hunted in Zululand? Ay, I will come.'

'Remember,' I said, 'if thou comest with us, we fight not save in self-defence. Listen, we need servants. These men,' and I pointed to the Wakwafi, 'say they will not come.'

'Will not come!' shouted Umslopogaas. 'Here, thou' – and with a single bound he sprang upon the Wakwafi with whom I had first spoken, and, seizing him by the arm, dragged him towards us. 'Thou dog!' he said, giving the terrified man a shake, 'didst thou say that thou wouldst not go with my Father? Say it once more and I will choke thee' – and his long fingers closed round his throat as he said it – 'thee, and those with thee. Hast thou forgotten how I served thy brother?'

'Nay, we will come with the great white chief,' gasped the man.

'So!' said Umslopogaas, in a quiet voice, as he suddenly released his hold, so that the man fell backward. 'I thought you would.'

'That man Umslopogaas seems to have a curious *moral* ascendency over his companions,' Good afterwards remarked thoughtfully.

TWO
The Black Hand

In due course we left Lamu, and ten days afterwards we found ourselves at a spot called Charra, on the Tana River. We had a violent quarrel with the headman of the bearers we had hired to go as far as this, and who now wished to extort large extra payment from us. In the result he threatened to set the Masai on to us. That night he, with all our hired bearers, ran away. So that we could continue, Good suggested that we bought canoes, to paddle up the river, and set to work to buy suitable ones from the surrounding natives. I succeeded after a delay of three days in obtaining two large ones, each hollowed out of a single log of some light wood, and capable of holding six people and baggage.

On the day following our purchase of the two canoes we effected a start. In the first canoe were Good, Sir Henry, and three of our Wakwafi followers; in the second myself, Umslopogaas, and the other two Wakwafis. As our course lay up stream, we had to keep four paddles at work in each canoe, which meant that the whole lot of us, except Good, had to row away like galley-slaves.

After the first day Good succeeded, with the help of some cloth and a couple of poles, in rigging up a sail in each canoe, which lightened our labours not a little. But the current ran very strong against us, and at the best we were not able to make more than twenty miles a day.

Three days after our start an ominous incident occurred. We were just drawing in to the bank to make our camp as usual for the night, when we caught sight of a figure standing on a little knoll not forty yards away, and intently watching our approach. One glance was sufficient – although I was personally unacquainted with the tribe – to tell me that he was a Masai Elmoran, or young warrior. Indeed, had I had any doubts, they would have quickly been dispelled by the terrified ejaculation of '*Masai!*' that burst simultaneously from the lips of our Wakwafi followers.

Whilst we were hesitating what to do, the Masai warrior drew himself up in a dignified fashion, shook his huge spear at us, and, turning, vanished on the further side of the slope.

'Hulloa!' holloaed Sir Henry from the other boat; 'our friend the caravan leader has been as good as his word, and set the Masai after us. Do you think it will be safe to go ashore?'

I did not think it would be at all safe; but, on the other hand, we had no means of cooking in the canoes, and nothing that we could eat raw, so it was difficult to know what to do. At last Umslopogaas simplified matters by volunteering to go and reconnoitre, which he did, creeping off into the bush like a snake, while we hung off in the stream waiting for him. In half an hour he returned, and told us that he had searched high and low and there was not a Masai to be seen anywhere about.

Thereupon we landed; and, having posted a sentry, proceeded to cook and eat our evening meal. However after eating we did not consider it safe to sleep ashore, so we got into our canoes, and, paddling out into the middle of the stream, which was not very wide here, managed to anchor them by means of big stones fastened to ropes made of cocoanut-fibre, of which there were several fathoms in each canoe.

Here the musquitoes nearly ate us up alive, and this, combined with anxiety as to our position, effectually prevented me from sleeping as the others were doing. And so I lay awake, smoking and reflecting on many things, but, being of a practical turn of mind, chiefly on how we were to give those Masai villains the slip. On looking towards the bank on our right, I fancied that I caught sight of a dark figure flitting between the tree trunks. I have very keen sight, and I was almost sure that I saw something, but whether it was bird, beast, or man I could not say. At that moment, however, a dark cloud passed over the moon, and I saw no more of it. Just then, too, although all the other sounds of the forest had ceased, a species of horned owl with which I was well acquainted began to hoot with great persistency. After that, save for the rustling of trees and reeds when the wind caught them, there was complete silence.

But somehow, in the most unaccountable way, I had suddenly become nervous. There was no particular reason why I should be, beyond the ordinary reasons which surround the Central African traveller, and yet I undoubtedly was. Worse and worse I grew, my pulse fluttered like a dying man's, my nerves thrilled with the horrible sense of impotent terror which anybody who is subject to nightmare will be familiar with, but still my will triumphed over my fears, and I lay quiet (for I was half sitting, half lying, in the bow of the canoe), only turning my face so as to command a view of Umslopogaas and the two Wakwafi who were sleeping alongside of and beyond me.

In the distance I heard a hippopotamus splash faintly, then the owl hooted again in a kind of unnatural screaming note. I afterwards learnt that the hooting of an owl is a signal among the Masai tribes. The wind began to moan plaintively through the trees, making a heart-chilling music. Above was the black bosom of the cloud, and beneath me swept the black flood of the water, and I felt as though I and Death were utterly alone between them. It was very desolate.

Suddenly my blood seemed to freeze in my veins, and my heart to stand still. Was it fancy, or were we moving? I turned my eyes to look for the other canoe which should be alongside of us. I could not see it, but instead I saw a lean and clutching black hand lifting itself above the gunwale of the little boat. Surely it was a nightmare! At the same instant a dim but devilish-looking face appeared to rise out of the water, and then came a lurch of the canoe, the quick flash of a knife, and an awful yell from the Wakwafi who was sleeping by my side and something warm spurted into my face. In an instant the spell was broken; I knew that it was no nightmare, but that we were attacked by swimming Masai. Snatching at the first weapon that came to hand, which happened to be Umslopogaas's battle-axe, I struck with all my force in the direction in which I had seen the flash of the knife. The blow fell upon a man's arm, and catching it against the thick wooden gunwale of the canoe, completely severed it from the body just above the wrist. As for its owner, he uttered no sound or cry. Like a ghost he came, and like a ghost he went, leaving behind him a bloody hand still gripping a great knife, or rather a short sword, that was buried in the heart of our poor servant.

Instantly there arose a hubbub and confusion, and I fancied, rightly or wrongly, that I made out several dark heads gliding away towards the right-hand bank, whither we were rapidly drifting, for the rope by which we were moored had been severed with a knife. As soon as I had realized this fact, I also realized that the scheme had been to cut the boat loose so that it should drift on to the right bank (as it would have done with the natural swing of the current), where no doubt a party of Masai were waiting to dig their shovel-headed spears into us. Seizing one paddle myself, I told Umslopogaas to take another (for the remaining Askari was too frightened and bewildered to be of any .use), and together we rowed vigorously out towards the middle of the stream; and not an instant too soon, for in another minute we should have been aground, and then there would have been an end of us.

As soon as we were well out, we set to work to paddle the canoe up stream again to where the other was moored; and very hard and dangerous work it was in the dark, and with nothing but the notes of Good's stentorian shouts, which he kept firing off at intervals like a fog-horn, to guide us. But at last we fetched up, and were thankful to find that they had not been molested at all. No doubt the owner of the same hand that severed our rope should have severed theirs also, but was led away from his purpose by an irresistible inclination to murder when he got the chance, which, whilst it cost us a man and him his hand, undoubtedly saved all the rest of us from massacre. Had it not been for that ghastly apparition over the side of the boat – an apparition that I shall never forget till my dying hour – the canoe would undoubtedly have drifted ashore before I realized what had happened, and this history would never have been written by me.

THREE
The Mission Station

We made the remains of our rope fast to the other canoe, and sat waiting for the dawn and congratulating ourselves upon our merciful escape, which really seemed to result more from the special favour of Providence than from our own care or prowess. At last it came, and I have not often been more grateful to see the light, though so far as my canoe was concerned it revealed a ghastly sight. There in the bottom of the little boat lay the unfortunate Askari, the sime, or sword, in his bosom, and the severed hand gripping the handle. I could not bear the sight, so hauling up the stone which had served as an anchor to the other canoe, we made it fast to the murdered man and dropped him overboard, and down he went to the bottom, leaving nothing but a train of bubbles behind him. The hand of his murderer we threw into the stream, where it slowly sank. The sword, of which the handle was ivory, inlaid with gold (evidently Arab work), I kept and used as a hunting-knife, and very useful it proved.

Then, a man having been transferred to my canoe, we once more started on in very low spirits and not feeling at all comfortable as to the future, but fondly hoping to arrive at the 'Highlands' station by night. To make matters worse, within an hour of sunrise it came on to rain in torrents, wetting us to the skin, and even necessitating the occasional baling of the canoes, and as the rain beat down the wind we could not use the sails, and had to get along as best we could with our paddles.

Just as we were thinking of halting to rest and try to shoot something to eat, a sudden bend in the river brought us in sight of a substantial-looking European house with a verandah round it, splendidly situated upon a hill, and surrounded by a high stone wall with a ditch on the outer side. Right against and overshadowing the house was an enormous pine, the top of which we had seen through a glass for the last two days, but of course without knowing that it marked the site of the mission station. I was the first to see the house, and could not restrain myself from giving a hearty cheer, in which the others, including the natives, joined lustily. Running the canoes to the bank, we disembarked, and were just hauling them up on to the shore, when we perceived three figures, dressed in ordinary English-looking clothes, hurrying down through a grove of trees to meet us.

'A gentleman, a lady, and a little girl,' ejaculated Good, after surveying the trio through his eyeglass, 'walking in a civilized fashion, through a civilized garden, to meet us in this place. Hang me, if this isn't the most curious thing we have seen yet!'

Good was right: it certainly did seem odd and out of place – more like a scene out of a dream or an Italian opera than a real tangible fact; and the sense of unreality was not lessened when we heard ourselves addressed in good broad Scotch.

'How do you do, sirs,' said Mr Mackenzie, a grey-haired, angular man, with a kindly face and red cheeks; 'I hope I see you very well. My natives told me an hour ago they spied two canoes with white men in them coming up the river; so we have just come down to meet you.'

'And it is very glad that we are to see you,' put in the lady – a charming and refined-looking person.

We took off our hats in acknowledgment, and proceeded to introduce ourselves.

'And now,' said Mr Mackenzie, 'you must all be hungry and weary; so come on up to our house, gentlemen.'

The house, a massively built single-storied building, was roofed with slabs of stone, and had a handsome verandah in front. It was built on three sides of a square, the fourth side being taken up by the kitchens, which stood separate from the house – a very good plan in a hot country. In the centre of this square thus formed was perhaps, the most remarkable object that we had yet seen in this charming place, and that was a single tree of the conifer tribe, varieties of which grow freely on the highlands of this part of Africa. This splendid tree, which Mr Mackenzie informed us was a landmark for fifty miles round, and which we had ourselves seen for the last forty miles of our journey, must have been nearly three hundred feet in height, the trunk measuring about sixteen feet in diameter at a yard from the ground.

'What a beautiful tree!' exclaimed Sir Henry.

'Yes, you are right; it is a beautiful tree. There is not another like it in all the country round, that I know of,' answered Mr Mackenzie. 'I call it my watch tower. As you see, I have a rope ladder fixed to the lowest bough; and if I want to see anything that is going on within fifteen miles or so, all I have to do is to run up it with a spyglass. But you must be hungry, and I am sure the dinner is cooked. Come in, my friends; it is but a rough place, but well enough for these savage parts; and I can tell you what, we have got – a French cook.' And he led the way on to the verandah.

As I was following him there suddenly appeared, through

the door that opened on to the verandah from the house, a dapper little man, dressed in a neat blue cotton suit, with shoes made of tanned hide, and remarkable for a bustling air and most enormous black mustachios, shaped into an upward curve, and coming to a point for all the world like a pair of buffalo-horns.

'Madame bids me for to say that dinner is sarved. Messieurs, my compliments;' then suddenly perceiving Umslopogaas, who was loitering along after us and playing with his battle-axe, he threw up his hands in astonishment. '*Ah, mais quel homme!*' he ejaculated in French, '*quel sauvage affreux!* Take but note of his huge choppare and the great pit in his head.'

'Ay,' said Mr Mackenzie; 'what are you talking about, Alphonse?'

'Talking about!' replied the little Frenchman, his eyes still fixed upon Umslopogaas, whose general appearance seemed to fascinate him; 'why I talk of him' – and he rudely pointed – 'of *ce monsieur noir*.'

At this everybody began to laugh, and Umslopogaas, perceiving that he was the object of remark, frowned ferociously, for he had a most lordly dislike of anything like a personal liberty.

'*Parbleu!*' said Alphonse, 'he is angered – he makes the grimace. I like not his air. I vanish.' And he did with considerable rapidity.

Mr Mackenzie joined heartily in the shout of laughter which we indulged in. 'He is a queer character – Alphonse,' he said. 'By-and-by I will tell you his history; in the meanwhile let us try his cooking.'

When dinner was over we lit our pipes, and Sir Henry proceeded to give our host a description of our journey up here, over which he looked very grave.

'It is evident to me,' he said, 'that those rascally Masai are following you, and I am very thankful that you have reached this house in safety. I do not think that they will dare to attack you here. It is unfortunate, though, that nearly all my men have gone down to the coast with ivory and goods. There are two hundred of them in the caravan, and the consequence is that I have not more than twenty men available for defensive purposes in case they should attack us.'

'I am sure I devoutly hope that we shall bring no such calamity upon you,' said I, anxiously, when he had taken his seat again. 'Rather than bring those bloodthirsty villains about your ears, we will move on and take our chance.'

'You will do nothing of the sort. If the Masai come, they come, and there is an end on it; and I think we can give them a pretty warm greeting. I would not show any man the door for all the Masai in the world.'

'That reminds me,' I said, 'the Consul at Lamu told me that he had had a letter from you, in which you said that a man had arrived here who reported that he had come across a white people in the interior. Do you think that there was any truth in his story?'

Mr Mackenzie, by way of answer, went out of the room and returned, bringing with him a most curious sword. It was long, and all the blade, which was very thick and heavy, was to within a quarter of an inch of the cutting edge worked into an ornamental pattern exactly as we work soft wood with a fret-saw, the steel, however, being invariably pierced in such a way as not to interfere with the strength of the sword. This in itself was sufficiently curious, but what was still more so was that all the edges of the hollow spaces cut through the substance of the blade were most beautifully inlaid with gold, which was in some way that I cannot understand welded on to the steel.

'There,' said Mr Mackenzie, 'did you ever see a sword like that?'

We all examined it and shook our heads.

'Well, I have got it to show you, because this is what the

man who said he had seen the white people brought with him, and because it does more or less give an air of truth to what I should otherwise have set down as a lie. Look here; I will tell you all that I know about the matter, which is not much. One afternoon, just before sunset, I was sitting on the verandah, when a poor, miserable, starved-looking man came limping up and squatted down before me. I asked him where he came from and what he wanted, and thereon he plunged into a long rambling narrative about how he belonged to a tribe far in the north, and how his tribe was destroyed by another tribe, and he with a few other survivors driven still further north past a lake named Laga. Thence, it appears, he made his way to another lake that lay up in the mountains, "a lake without a bottom" he called it, and here his wife and brother died of an infectious sickness – probably smallpox – whereon the people drove him out of their villages into the wilderness, where he wandered miserably over mountains for ten days, after which he got into dense thorn forest, and was one day found there by some *white men* who were hunting, and who took him to a place where all the people were white and lived in stone houses. Here he remained a week shut up in a house, till one night a man with a white beard, whom he understood to be a "medicine-man", came and inspected him, after which he was led off and taken through the thorn forest to the confines of the wilderness, and given food and this sword (at least so he said), and turned loose. Whether or not there is any truth in his story is more than I can tell you. What do you think, Mr Quatermain?'

I shook my head, and answered, 'I don't know. There are so many queer things hidden away in the heart of this great continent that I should be sorry to assert that there was no truth in it. Anyhow, we mean to try and find out.'

'You are very venturesome people,' said Mr Mackenzie, with a smile, and the subject dropped.

FOUR
Alphonse and his Annette

After dinner we thoroughly inspected all the outbuildings and grounds of the station, which I consider the most successful as well as the most beautiful place of the sort that I have seen in Africa. We then returned to the verandah, where we found Umslopogaas taking advantage of this favourable opportunity to clean all the rifles thoroughly. This was the only *work* that he ever did or was asked to do, for as a Zulu chief it was beneath his dignity to work with his hands; but such as it was he did it very well. It was a curious sight to see the great Zulu sitting there upon the floor, his battle-axe resting against the wall behind him, whilst his long aristocratic-looking hands were busily employed, delicately and with the utmost care, cleaning the mechanism of the breechloaders.

He also cleaned his battle-axe, which he seemed to look upon as an intimate friend, and to which he would at times talk by the hour, going over all his old adventures with it – and dreadful enough some of them were. By a piece of grim humour, he had named this axe 'Inkosi-kaas', which is the

Zulu word for chieftainess. For a long while I could not make out why he gave it such a name, and at last I asked him, when he informed me that the axe was evidently feminine, because of her womanly habit of prying very deep into things, and that she was clearly a chieftainess because all men fell down before her, struck dumb at the sight of her beauty and power. In the same way he would consult 'Inkosi-kaas' if in any dilemma; and when I asked him why he did so, he informed me it was because she must needs be wise, having 'looked into so many people's brains'.

I took up the axe and closely examined this formidable weapon. The cutting part was slightly concave in shape – not convex, as is generally the case with savage battle-axes – and sharp as a razor, measuring five and three-quarter inches across the widest part. From the back of the axe sprang a stout spike four inches long, for the last two of which it was hollow, and shaped like a leather punch, with an opening for anything forced into the hollow at the punch end to be pushed out above. It was with this punch end, as we afterwards discovered, that Umslopogaas usually struck when fighting, driving a neat round hole in his adversary's skull, and only using the broad cutting edge for a circular sweep, or sometimes in a *mêlée*. I think he considered the punch a neater and more sportsmanlike tool, and it was from his habit of pecking at his enemy with it that he got his name of 'Woodpecker'. Certainly in his hands it was a terribly efficient one.

Just as I returned his axe to Umslopogaas, Miss Flossie, Mr Mackenzie's little daughter, came up and took me off to see her collection of flowers. African liliums, and blooming shrubs, some of which are very beautiful, many of the varieties being quite unknown to me and also, I believe, to botanical science. I asked her if she had ever seen or heard of the 'Goya' lily, which Central African explorers have told me they have occasionally met with and whose wonderful loveliness has filled them with astonishment. To my great delight Miss Flossie told me that she knew the flower well and had tried to grow it in her garden, but without success, adding, however, that as it should be in bloom at this time of year she thought that she could procure me a specimen.

After that I fell to asking her if she was not lonely up here among all these savage people and without any companions of her own age.

'Lonely?' she said. 'Oh, indeed no! I am as happy as the day is long, and besides I have my own companions. I have read about little girls in England. Everybody thinks them a trouble, and they have to do what their schoolmistress likes. Oh! it would break my heart to be put in a cage like that and not to be free – free as the air.'

'Would you not like to learn?' I asked.

'So I do learn. Father teaches me Latin and French and arithmetic.'

'And are you never afraid here?'

'Afraid? Oh no! Look here,' and diving her little hand into the bodice of her dress she produced a double-barrelled nickel-plated Derringer, 'I always carry that loaded, and if anybody tried to touch me I should shoot him. Once I shot a leopard that jumped upon my donkey as I was riding along. It frightened me very much, but I shot it in the ear and it fell dead, and I have its skin upon my bed.'

Just then the spies whom our host had sent out in the morning to find out if there were any traces of our Masai friends about, returned, and reported that the country had been scoured for fifteen miles round without a single Elmoran being seen.

After the spies had gone, and Mrs Mackenzie and Flossie had retired for the night, Alphonse, the little Frenchman, came out, and Sir Henry, who is a very good French scholar, got him to tell us how he came to visit Central

Africa, which he did in a most extraordinary lingo, that for the most part I shall not attempt to reproduce.

'I am, messieurs, a cook, and I was born at Marseilles. In that dear town I spent my happy youth. For years and years I washed the dishes at the Hôtel Continental. Ah, those were golden days!' and he sighed. 'I am a Frenchman. Need I say, messieurs, that I admire beauty? Nay, I adore the fair. Messieurs, we admire all the roses in a garden, but we pluck one. *I* plucked one, and alas, messieurs, it pricked my finger. She was a chambermaid, her name Annette, her figure ravishing, her face an angel's. I loved to desperation, I adored her to despair. Never have I cooked as I cooked (for I had been promoted at the hotel) when Annette, my adored Annette, smiled on me. We loved, and were happy in each other's love. The birds in their little nest could not be happier than Alphonse and his Annette. Then came the blow. I was drawn for the conscription. The evil moment came; I had to go. I had a cousin a linendraper, well-to-do, but very ugly. "To thee, my cousin," I said, "I consign Annette. Watch over her whilst I hunt for glory in the bloody field."

'"Make your mind easy," said he; "I will." As the sequel shows, he did!

'I went. I lived in barracks on black soup. I am a refined man and a poet by nature, and I suffered tortures from the coarse horror of my surroundings. So I deserted.

'I reached Marseilles disguised as an old man. I went to the house of my cousin – and there sat Annette. It was the season of cherries. They took a double stalk. At each end was a cherry. My cousin put one into his mouth, Annette put the other in hers. Then they drew the stalks in till their lips met – and alas, alas that I should have to say it! – they kissed. The game was a pretty one, but the heroic blood of my grandfather, a soldier who served under Napoleon, boiled up in me. I rushed into the kitchen. I struck my cousin with the old man's crutch. He fell – I had slain him.

'Annette screamed. The gendarmes came. I fled. I reached the harbour. I hid aboard a vessel. The vessel put to sea. The captain found me and beat me.

'He did not put me ashore because I cooked well. I cooked for him all the way to Zanzibar, where I escaped. I fled, I starved. I met the men of Monsieur le Curé. They brought me here. I am here full of woe. But I return not to France. Better to risk my life in these horrible places than to know the Bagne.'

He paused, and none of us knew quite what to say. 'Perhaps,' said Sir Henry, at last, 'the heroic blood of your grandparent will triumph after all; perhaps you will still be great. At any rate we shall see. And now I vote we go to bed. I am dead tired, and we had not much sleep last night.'

And so we did, and very strange the tidy rooms and clean white sheets seemed to us after our recent experiences.

FIVE
Umslopogaas Makes a Promise

Next morning at breakfast I missed Flossie and asked where she was.

'Well,' said her mother, 'when I got up this morning I found a note put outside my door in which—But here it is, you can read it for yourself,' and she gave me the slip of paper on which the following was written: –

'DEAREST M—, – It is just dawn, and I am off to the hills to get Mr Q— a bloom of the lily he wants, so don't expect me till you see me. I have taken the white donkey; and nurse and a couple of boys are coming with me – also something to eat, as I may be away all day, for I am determined to get the lily if I have to go twenty miles for it. – FLOSSIE.'

'I hope she will be all right,' I said, a little anxiously; 'I never meant her to trouble after the flower.'

'Ah, Flossie can look after herself,' said her mother; 'she often goes off in this way like a true child of the wilderness.'

But Mr Mackenzie, who came in just then and saw the note for the first time, looked rather grave, though he said nothing.

After breakfast was over I took him aside and asked him if it would not be possible to send after the girl and get her back, having in view the possibility of there still being some Masai hanging about, at whose hands she might come to harm.

'I fear it would be of no use,' he answered. 'She may be fifteen miles off by now, and it is impossible to say what path she has taken. There are the hills;' and he pointed to a long range of rising ground stretching almost parallel with the course followed by the river Tana, but gradually sloping down to a dense bush-clad plain about five miles short of the house.

Here I suggested that we might get up the great tree over the house and search the country round with a spyglass; and this, after Mr Mackenzie had given some orders to his people to try and follow Flossie's spoor, we did.

The view was simply glorious. In every direction the bush rolled away in great billows for miles and miles, as far as the glass would show, only here and there broken by the brighter green of patches of cultivation, or by the glittering surfaces of lakes. To the north-west Mt Kenia reared his mighty head, and we could trace the Tana River curling like a silver snake.

But look as we would, we could see no signs of Flossie and her donkey, so at last had to come down disappointed. On reaching the verandah I found Umslopogaas sitting there, slowly and lightly sharpening his axe with a small whetstone he always carried with him.

'What doest thou, Umslopogaas?' I asked.

'I smell blood,' was the answer; and I could get no more out of him.

After dinner we again went up the tree and searched the

surrounding country with a spyglass, but without result. When we came down Umslopogaas was still sharpening Inkosi-kaas, although she already had an edge like a razor. Standing in front of him, and regarding him with a mixture of fear and fascination, was Alphonse. And certainly he did seem an alarming object – sitting there, Zulu fashion, on his haunches, a wild look upon his intensely savage and yet intellectual face, sharpening, sharpening, sharpening at the murderous-looking axe.

'Oh, the monster, the horrible man!' said the little French cook, lifting his hands in amazement. 'See but the hole in his head; the skin beats on it up and down like a baby's! Who would nurse such a baby?' and he burst out laughing at the idea.

For a moment Umslopogaas looked up from his sharpening, and a sort of evil light played in his dark eyes.

'What does the little "buffalo-heifer" (so named by Umslopogaas, on account of his mustachios and feminine characteristics) say? Let him be careful, or I will cut his horns. Beware, little man monkey, beware!'

Unfortunately Alphonse, who was getting over his fear of him, went on laughing at '*ce drôle d'un monsieur noir*'. I was about to warn him to desist, when suddenly the huge Zulu bounded off the verandah on to the open space where Alphonse was standing, his features alive with a sort of malicious enthusiasm, and began swinging the axe round and round over the Frenchman's head.

'Stand still,' I shouted; 'do not move as you value your life – he will not hurt you;' but I doubt if Alphonse heard me, being, fortunately for himself, almost petrified with horror.

Then followed the most extraordinary display of sword, or rather of axemanship, that I ever saw. First of all the axe went flying round and round over the top of Alphonse's head, with an angry whirl and such extraordinary swiftness that it looked like a continuous band of steel, ever getting nearer and yet nearer to that unhappy individual's skull, till at last it grazed it as it flew. Then suddenly the motion was changed, and it seemed to literally flow up and down his body and limbs, never more than an eighth of an inch from them, and yet never striking them. It was a wonderful sight to see the little man fixed there, having apparently realized that to move would be to run the risk of sudden death, while his black tormentor towered over him, and wrapped him round with the quick flashes of the axe. For a minute or more this went on, till suddenly I saw the moving brightness travel down the side of Alphonse's face, and then outwards and stop. As it did so a tuft of something black fell to the ground; it was the tip of one of the little Frenchman's curling mustachios.

Umslopogaas leant upon the handle of Inkosi-kaas, and broke into a long, low laugh; and Alphonse, overcome with fear, sank into a sitting posture on the ground, whilst we stood astonished at this exhibition of almost superhuman skill and mastery of a weapon. 'Inkosi-kaas is sharp enough,' he shouted; 'the blow that clipped the "buffalo-heifer's" horn would have split a man from the crown to the chin. Few could have struck it but I; none could have struck it and not taken off the shoulder too. Look, thou little heifer! Am I a good man to laugh at, thinkest thou? For a space hast thou stood within a hair's-breadth of death. Laugh not again, lest the hair's-breadth be wanting. I have spoken.'

'What meanest thou by such mad tricks?' I asked of Umslopogaas, indignantly. 'Surely thou art mad. Twenty times didst thou go near to slaying the man.'

'And yet, Macumazahn, I slew not. Now I go to make a shield, for I smell blood.'

'That is an uncomfortable sort of retainer of yours,' said

Mr Mackenzie, who had witnessed this extraordinary scene.

'He says he smells blood. I only trust he is not right. I am getting very fearful about my little girl. She must have gone far, or she would be home by now. It is half-past three o'clock.'

After this the afternoon wore drearily on, and towards evening, there still being no signs of Flossie, our anxiety grew very keen. As for the poor mother, she was quite prostrated by her fears, and no wonder, but the father kept his head wonderfully well. Everything that could be done was done: people were sent out in all directions, shots were fired, and a continuous outlook kept from the great tree, but without avail.

And then at last it grew dark, and still no sign of fair-haired little Flossie.

At eight o'clock we had supper. It was but a sorrowful meal, and Mrs Mackenzie did not appear at it.

When supper was nearly at an end I made an excuse to leave the table. I wanted to get outside and think the situation over. I went on to the verandah and, having lit my pipe, sat down on a seat.

I had been sitting there perhaps six or seven minutes when I thought I heard the door move. I looked in that direction and listened, but, being unable to make out anything, concluded that I must have been mistaken. It was a darkish night, the moon not having yet risen.

Another minute passed, when suddenly something round fell with a soft but heavy thud upon the stone flooring of the verandah, and came bounding and rolling along past me. For a moment I did not rise, but sat wondering what it could be. Finally, I concluded it must have been an animal. Just then, however, another idea struck me, and I got up quick enough. The thing lay quite still a few feet beyond me. I put down my hand towards it and it did not move:

clearly it was not an animal. My hand touched it. It was soft and warm and heavy. Hurriedly I lifted it and held it up against the faint starlight.

It was a newly severed human head!

I am an old hand and not easily upset, but I own that that ghastly sight made me feel sick. How had the thing come there? Whose was it? I put it down and ran to the little doorway. I could see nothing, hear nobody. I was about to go out into the darkness beyond, but remembering that to do so was to expose myself to the risk of being stabbed, I drew back, shut the door, and bolted it. Then I returned to the verandah, and in as careless a voice as I could command called Curtis. I fear, however, that my tones must have betrayed me, for not only Sir Henry but also Good and Mackenzie rose from the table and came hurrying out.

'What is it?' said the clergyman, anxiously.

Then I had to tell them.

Mr Mackenzie turned pale as death under his red skin. We were standing opposite the hall door, and there was a light in it so that I could see. He snatched the head up by the hair and held it against the light.

'It is the head of one of the men who accompanied Flossie,' he said with a gasp. 'Thank God it is not hers!'

We all stood and stared at each other aghast. What was to be done?

Just then there was a knocking at the door that I had bolted, and a voice cried, 'Open, my father, open!'

The door was unlocked, and in sped a terrified man. He was one of the spies who had been sent out.

'My father,' he cried, 'the Masai are on us! A great body of them have passed round the hill and are moving towards the old stone kraal down by the little stream. My father, make strong thy heart! In the midst of them I saw the white ass, and on it sat the Waterlily [Flossie].'

'Was the child alive?' asked Mr Mackenzie, hoarsely.

'She was white as the snow, but well, my father. They passed quite close to me, and looking up from where I lay hid I saw her face against the sky.'

'God help her and us!' groaned the clergyman.

'How many are there of them?' I asked.

'More than two hundred – two hundred and half a hundred.'

Once more we looked one on the other. What was to be done? Just then there rose a loud insistent cry outside the wall.

'Open the door, white man; open the door! A herald – a herald to speak with thee.' Thus cried the voice.

Umslopogaas ran to the wall, and, reaching with his long arms to the coping, lifted his head above it and gazed over.

'I see but one man,' he said. 'He is armed, and carries a basket in his hand.'

'Open the door,' I said. 'Umslopogaas, take thine axe and stand thereby. Let one man pass. If another follows, slay.'

The door was unbarred. In the shadow of the wall stood Umslopogaas, his axe raised above his head to strike. Just then the moon came out. There was a moment's pause, and then in stalked a Masai Elmoran.

When he got opposite to us he halted, put down the basket, and stuck the spike of his spear into the ground, so that it stood upright.

'Let us talk,' he said. 'The first messenger we sent to you could not talk;' and he pointed to the head which lay upon the paving of the step – a ghastly sight in the moonlight; 'but I have words to speak if ye have ears to hear. Also I bring presents;' and he pointed to the basket and laughed with an air of swaggering insolence that is perfectly indescribable, and yet which one could not but admire, seeing that he was surrounded by enemies.

'Say on,' said Mr Mackenzie.

'I am the "Lygonani" [war captain] of a part of the Masai

of the Guasa Amboni. I and my men followed these three white men,' and he pointed to Sir Henry, Good, and myself, 'but they were too clever for us, and escaped hither. We have a quarrel with them, and are going to kill them.'

'Are you, my friend?' said I to myself.

'In following these men we this morning caught two black men, one black woman, a white donkey, and a white girl. One of the black men we killed – there is his head upon the pavement; the other ran away. The black woman, the little white girl, and the white ass we took and brought with us. In proof thereof have I brought this basket that she carried. Is it not thy daughter's basket?'

Mr Mackenzie nodded, and the warrior went on.

'Good! With thee and thy daughter we have no quarrel, nor do we wish to harm thee, save as to thy cattle, which we have already gathered, two hundred and forty head – a beast for every man's father.'

Here Mr Mackenzie gave a groan, as he greatly valued this herd of cattle, which he bred with much care and trouble.

'So, save for the cattle, thou mayest go free; more especially,' he added frankly, glancing at the wall, 'as this place would be a difficult one to take. But as to these men it is otherwise; we have followed them for nights and days, and must kill them. Were we to return to our kraal without having done so, all the girls would make a mock of us. So, however troublesome it may be, they must die.

'Now I have a proposition for thine ear. We would not harm the little girl; she is too fair to harm, and has besides a brave spirit. Give us one of these three men – a life for a life – and we will let her go, and throw in the black woman with her also. This is a fair offer, white man. We ask but for one, not for the three; we must take another opportunity to kill the other two. I do not even pick my man, though I should prefer the big one,' pointing to Sir Henry; 'he looks strong, and would die more slowly.'

'And if I say I will not yield the man?' said Mr Mackenzie.

'Nay, say not so, white man,' answered the Masai, 'for then thy daughter dies at dawn, and the woman with her says thou hast no other child. Were she older I would take her for a servant; but as she is so young I will slay her with my own hand – ay, with this very spear. Thou canst come and see, an' thou wilt. I give thee a safe conduct;' and the fiend laughed aloud at his brutal jest.

Meanwhile I had been thinking rapidly, as one does in emergencies, and had come to a conclusion.

'All right, Mackenzie,' I said, 'you can tell the man that I will exchange myself against Flossie, only I stipulate that she shall be safely in this house before they kill me.'

'Eh?' said Sir Henry and Good simultaneously. 'That you don't.'

'No, no,' said Mr Mackenzie, 'I will have no man's blood upon my hands. If it please God that my daughter die this awful death, His will be done. You are a brave man (which I am not by any means) and a noble man, Quatermain, but you shall not go.'

'If nothing else turns up I shall go,' I said decidedly.

'This is an important matter,' said Mackenzie, addressing the Lygonani, 'and we must think it over. You shall have our answer at dawn.'

'Very well, white man,' answered the savage indifferently; 'only remember if thy answer is late thy little white bud will never grow into a flower, that is all, for I shall cut it with this,' and he touched the spear. 'I should have thought that thou wouldst play a trick and attack us at night, but I know from the woman with the girl that your men are down at the coast, and that thou hast but twenty men here.' Then turning to Umslopogaas, who had all the while been standing behind him and shepherding him as it were, 'Open the door for me, fellow, quick now.'

This was too much for the old chief's patience. For the last ten minutes his lips had been figuratively speaking, positively watering over the Masai Lygonani, and this he could not stand. Placing his long hand on the Elmoran's shoulder he gripped it and gave him such a twist as brought him face to face with himself. Then, thrusting his fierce countenance to within a few inches of the Masai's evil feather-framed features, he said in a low growling voice: —

'Seest thou me?'

'Ay, fellow, I see thee.'

'And seest thou this?' and he held Inkosi-kaas before his eyes.

'Ay, fellow, I see the toy; what of it?'

'Thou Masai dog, thou boasting windbag, thou capturer of little girls, with this "toy" will I hew thee limb from limb. Well for thee that thou art a herald, or even now would I strew thy members about the grass.'

The Masai shook his great spear and laughed long and loud as he answered, 'I would that thou stoodst against me man to man, and we would see,' and again he turned to go, still laughing.

'Thou shalt stand against me man to man, be not afraid,' replied Umslopogaas, still in the same ominous voice. 'Ay, laugh on, laugh on! to-morrow night shall the jackals laugh as they crunch thy ribs.'

When the Lygonani had gone, one of us thought of opening the basket he had brought as a proof that Flossie was really their prisoner. On lifting the lid it was found to contain a most lovely specimen of both bulb and flower of the Goya lily, which I have already described, in full bloom and quite uninjured, and what was more a note in Flossie's childish hand written in pencil upon a greasy piece of paper that had been used to wrap up some food in: —

'DEAREST FATHER AND MOTHER,' ran the note, – 'The Masai caught us when we were coming home with the lily. I tried to escape but could not. They killed Tom: the other man ran away. They have not hurt nurse and me, but say that they mean to exchange us against one of Mr Quatermain's party. *I will have nothing of the sort.* Do not let anybody give his life for me. Try and attack them at night; they are going to feast on three bullocks they have stolen and killed. I have my pistol, and if no help comes by dawn I will shoot myself. They shall not kill me. If so, remember me always, dearest father and mother. I am very frightened, but I trust in God. I dare not write any more as they are beginning to notice. Good-bye. – FLOSSIE.'

Scrawled across the outside of this was 'Love to Mr Quatermain. They are going to take up the basket, so he will get the lily.'

When I read those words, written by that brave little girl in an hour of danger sufficiently near and horrible to have turned the brain of a strong man, I own I wept, and once more in my heart I vowed that she should not die while my life could be given to save her.

Then eagerly, quickly, almost fiercely, we fell to discussing the situation. Again I said that I would go, and again Mackenzie negatived it, and Curtis and Good, like the true men that they are, vowed that, if I did, they would go with me, and die back to back with me.

'It is,' I said at last, 'absolutely necessary that an effort of some sort should be made before the morning.'

'Then let us attack them with what force we can muster, and take our chance,' said Sir Henry.

'Ay, ay,' growled Umslopogaas, in Zulu; 'spoken like a man, Incubu. What is there to be afraid of? Two hundred and fifty Masai, forsooth! How many are we? The chief there [Mr Mackenzie] has twenty men, and thou, Macumazahn, hast five men, and there are also five white men – that is thirty men in all – enough, enough. Listen now, Macumazahn, thou who are very clever and old in war. What says the maid? These men eat and make merry; let it be their funeral feast. What said the dog whom I hope to hew down at daybreak? That he feard no attack because we were so few. Knowest thou the old kraal where the men have camped? I saw it this morning; it is thus;' and he drew an oval on the floor; 'here is the big entrance, filled up with thorn bushes, and opening on to a steep rise. Why, Incubu, thou and I with axes will hold it against an hundred men striving to break out! Look, now; thus shall the battle go. Just as the light begins to glint upon the oxen's horns – not before, or it will be too dark, and not later, or they will be awakening and perceive us – let Bougwan creep round with ten men to the top end of the kraal, where the narrow entrance is. Let them silently slay the sentry there so that he makes no sound, and stand ready. Then, Incubu, let thee and me and one of the Askari – the one with the broad chest – he is a brave man – creep to the wide entrance that is filled with thorn bushes, and there also slay the sentry, and armed with battle-axes take our stand also one on each side of the pathway, and one a few paces beyond to deal with such as pass the twain at the gate. It is there that the rush will come. That will have sixteen men. Let these men be divided into two parties, with one of which shalt thou go, Macumazahn, and with one the "praying man" [Mr Mackenzie], and, all armed with rifles, let them make their way one to the right side of the kraal and one to the left; and when thou, Macumazahn, lowest like an ox, all shall open fire with the guns upon the sleeping men, being very careful not to hit the little maid. Then shall Bougwan at the far end and his ten men raise their war-cry, and, springing over the wall, put the Masai there to the sword. And it shall happen that, being yet heavy with food and sleep, and bewildered by the firing of the guns, the falling of men, and the spears of

Bougwan, the soldiers shall rise and rush like wild game towards the thorn-stopped entrance, and there the bullets from either side shall plough through them, and there shall Incubu and the Askari and I wait for those who break across. Such is my plan, Macumazahn; if thou hast a better, name it.'

When he had done, I explained to the others such portions of this scheme as they had failed to understand, and they all joined with me in expressing the greatest admiration of the acute and skilful programme devised by the old Zulu, who was indeed the finest general I ever knew. After some discussion we determined to accept the scheme, as it stood, it being the only one possible under the circumstances, and giving the best chance of success that such a forlorn hope would admit of – which, however, considering the enormous odds and the character of our foe, was not very great.

'Ah, old lion!' I said to Umslopogaas, 'thou knowest how to lie in wait as well as how to bite, where to seize as well as where to hang on.'

'Ay, ay, Macumazahn,' he answered. 'For thirty years have I been a warrior, and have seen many things. It will be a good fight. I smell blood – I tell thee, I smell blood.'

SIX

The Night Wears On

Immediately after we had settled upon the outline of our plan of action as suggested by Umslopogaas, Mr Mackenzie sent for four sharp boys of from twelve to fifteen years of age, and despatched them to various points whence they could keep an outlook upon the Masai camp, with orders to report from time to time what was going on. Other lads and even women were stationed at intervals along the wall in order to guard against the possibility of surprise.

After this the twenty men who formed his whole available fighting force were summoned by our host into the square formed by the house, and there, standing by the bole of the great conifer, he earnestly addressed them and our four Askari.

'Men,' said Mr Mackenzie, after he had put all the circumstances of the case fully and clearly before them, and explained to them the proposed plan of our forlorn hope – 'men, for years I have been a good friend to you, protecting you, teaching you, guarding you and yours from harm, and ye have prospered with me. Ye have seen my child – the

Waterlily, as ye call her – grow year by year, from tenderest infancy to tender childhood, and from childhood on towards maidenhood. She has been your children's playmate, she has helped to tend you when sick, and ye have loved her.'

'We have,' said a deep voice, 'and we will die to save her.'

'I thank you from my heart – I thank you. Sure am I that now, in this hour of darkest trouble; now that her young life is like to be cut off by cruel and savage men – who of a truth "know now what they do" – ye will strive your best to save her, and to save me and her mother from broken hearts. Think, too, of your own wives and children. If she dies, her death will be followed by an attack upon us here, and at the best, even if we hold our own, your houses and gardens will be destroyed, and your goods and cattle swept away. I am, as ye well know, a man of peace. Never in all these years have I lifted my hand to shed man's blood; but now I say strike, strike, in the name of God, Who bade us protect our lives and homes.'

'Say no more, father,' said the same deep voice, that belonged to a stalwart elder of the Mission; 'we swear to save the Waterlily. May we and ours die the death of dogs, and our bones be thrown to the jackals and the kites, if we break the oath!'

'Ay, thus say we all,' chimed in the others.

'Thus say we all,' said I.

'It is well,' went on Mr Mackenzie. 'Ye are true men and not broken reeds to lean on. And now, friends – white and black together – let us kneel and offer up our humble prayers.'

And he knelt down, an example that we all followed, except Umslopogaas, who still stood in the background, grimly leaning on Inkosi-kaas. The fierce old Zulu had no gods and worshipped nought, unless it were his battle-axe.

After a moment's silence we all rose, and then began our

preparations in good earnest. As Umslopogaas said, it was
time to stop 'talking' and get to business. The men who
were to form each little party were carefully selected, and
still more carefully and minutely instructed as to what was
to be done. After much consideration it was agreed that the
ten men led by Good, whose duty it was to stampede the
camp, were not to carry firearms; that is, with the exception
of Good himself, who had a revolver as well as a short sword
– the Masai 'sime' which I had taken from the body of our
poor servant who was murdered in the canoe. We feared
that if they had firearms the result of three cross-fires
carried on at once would be that some of our own people
would be shot; besides, it appeared to all of us that the work
they had to do would best be carried out with the cold steel –
especially to Umslopogaas, who was, indeed, a great advo-
cate of cold steel. We had with us four Winchester repeating
rifles, beside half a dozen Martini rifles. I armed myself with
one of the repeaters – my own; an excellent weapon for this
kind of work, where great rapidity of fire is desirable. Mr
Mackenzie took another, and the two remaining ones were
given to two of his men who understood the use of them and
were noted shots. The Martinis and some rifles of Mr
Mackenzie's were served out, together with a plentiful
supply of ammunition, to the other natives who were to
form the two parties whose duty it was to be to open fire
from separate sides of the kraal on the sleeping Masai, and
who were fortunately all more or less accustomed to the use
of a gun.

As for Umslopogaas, we know how he was armed – with
an axe. It may be remembered that he, Sir Henry, and the
strongest of the Askari were to hold the thorn-stopped
entrance to the kraal against the anticipated rush of men
striving to escape. Of course, for such a purpose at this guns
were useless. Therefore Sir Henry and the Askari proceeded to arm themselves in like fashion. It so happened

that Mr Mackenzie had in his little store a selection of the very best steel English-made hammer-backed axes. Sir Henry selected one of these. When this important matter had been attended to, I went into my room and proceeded to open a little tin-lined deal case, which had not been undone since we left England, and which contained four mail shirts. These shirts, or rather steel-sleeved and high-necked jerseys, lined with ventilated wash leather, were not bright, but browned like a barrel of a gun; and mine fitted me so well that I found I could wear it for days next my skin without being chafed. Sir Henry had two. With these shirts were what looked like four brown cloth travelling caps with ear pieces. Each of these caps was, however, quilted with steel links so as to afford a most valuable protection for the head.

It seems almost laughable to talk of steel shirts in these days of bullets, against which they are of course quite useless; but where one has to do with savages, armed with cutting weapons such as assegais or battle-axes, they afford the most valuable protection. As Curtis had two I suggested that he should lend the other to Umslopogaas, who was to share the danger and the glory of his post. He readily consented, and called the Zulu, who came bearing Sir Henry's axe with him. When we showed him the steel shirt, and explained to him that we wanted him to wear it, he at first declined, saying that he had fought in his own skin for thirty years, and that he was not going to begin now to fight in an iron one. Thereupon I took a heavy spear, and, spreading the shirt upon the floor, drove the spear down upon it with all my strength, the weapon rebounded without leaving a mark upon the tempered steel. This exhibition half converted him; and when I pointed out to him how necessary it was that he should not let any old-fashioned prejudices he might possess stand in the way of a precaution which might preserve a valuable life at a time when men were scarce, and also that if he wore this shirt he might dispense with a shield, and so have both hands free, he yielded at once, and proceeded to invest his frame with the 'iron skin'.

As there was absolutely nothing further that could be done then we all took some supper, and went to lie down for a couple of hours. I could not help admiring the way in which old Umslopogaas flung himself upon the floor, and, unmindful of what was hanging over him, instantly sank into a deep sleep. I do not know how it was with the others, but I could not do as much. Indeed, as is usual with me on these occasions, I am sorry to say that I felt rather frightened; and, now that some of the enthusiasm had gone out of me, and I began to calmly contemplate what we had undertaken to do, truth compels me to add that I did not like it. We were but thirty men all told, a good many of whom were no doubt quite unused to fighting, and we were going to engage two hundred and fifty of the fiercest, bravest, and most formidable savages in Africa, who, to make matters worse, were protected by a stone wall. It was, indeed, a mad undertaking, and what made it even madder was the exceeding improbability of our being able to take up our positions without attracting the notice of the sentries. Of course if we once did that – and any slight accident, such as the chance discharge of a gun, might do it – we were done for, for the whole camp would be up in a second, and our only hope lay in a surprise.

Half past three came at last, and everybody was up and dressing. I put on a light jacket over my mail shirt in order to have a pocket handy to hold my cartridges, and buckled on my revolver. Good did the same, but Sir Henry put on nothing except his mail-shirt, steel-lined cap, and a pair of 'veldtschoons' or soft hide shoes, his legs being bare from the knees down. His revolver he strapped on round his middle outside the armoured shirt.

Meanwhile Umslopogaas was mustering the men in the square under the big tree and going the rounds to check and check again that each was properly armed.

SEVEN
A Slaughter Grim and Great

There was a long pause, and we stood there in the chilly silent darkness waiting till the moment came to start. It was, perhaps, the most trying time of all – that slow, slow quarter of an hour. The minutes seemed to drag along with leaden feet, and the quiet, the solemn hush, that brooded over all – big, as it were, with a coming fate, was most oppressive to the spirits.

The moon went down, for a long while she had been getting nearer and nearer to the horizon, now she finally sank and left the world in darkness save for a faint grey tinge in the eastern sky that palely heralded the dawn.

Mr Mackenzie stood, watch in hand, his wife clinging to his arm and striving to stifle her sobs.

'Twenty minutes to four,' he said, 'it ought to be light enough to attack at twenty minutes past four. Captain Good had better be moving, he will want three or four minutes' start.'

Good gave one final polish to his eyeglass, nodded to us in a jocular sort of way – which I could not help feeling it must have cost him something to muster up – and, ever polite, took off his steel-lined cap to Mrs Mackenzie and started for his position at the head of the kraal, to reach which he had to make a detour by some paths known to the natives.

The cattle kraal where the Masai were camped lay at the foot of the hill on which the house stood, or, roughly speaking, about eight hundred yards from the Mission buildings. The first five hundred yards of this distance we traversed quietly indeed, but at a good pace; after that we crept forward as silently as a lepoard on his prey, gliding like ghosts from bush to bush and stone to stone.

At last we were within fifty yards of the kraal. Between us and it was an open space of sloping grass with only one mimosa bush and a couple of tussocks of a sort of thistle for cover. We were still hidden in fairly thick bush. It was beginning to grow light. The stars had paled and a sickly gleam played about the east and was reflected on the earth. We could see the outline of the kraal clearly enough, and could also make out the faint glimmer of the dying embers of the Masai camp fires. We halted and watched, for the sentry we knew was posted at the opening. Presently he appeared, a fine tall fellow, walking idly up and down within five paces of the thorn-stopped entrance. We had hoped to catch him napping, but it was not to be. He seemed particularly wide awake. If we could not kill that man, and kill him silently, we were lost. There we crouched and watched him. Presently Umslopogaas, who was a few paces ahead of me, turned and made a sign, and next second I saw him go down on his stomach like a snake, and, taking an opportunity when the sentry's head was turned, begin to work his way through the grass without a sound.

The unconscious sentry commenced to hum a little tune, and Umslopogaas crept on. He reached the shelter of the mimosa bush unperceived and there waited. Still the sentry walked up and down. Presently he turned and looked over the wall into the camp. Instantly the human snake who was stalking him glided on ten yards and got behind one of the tussocks of the thistle-like plant, reaching it as the Elmoran turned again. As he did so his eye fell upon this patch of thistles, and it seemed to strike him that it did not look quite right. He advanced a pace towards it – halted, yawned, stooped down, picked up a little pebble and threw it at it. It hit Umslopogaas upon the head, luckily not upon the armour shirt. Had it done so the clink would have betrayed us. Luckily, too, the shirt was browned and not bright steel, which would certainly have been detected. Apparently satisfied that there was nothing wrong, he then gave over his investigations and contented himself with leaning on his spear and standing gazing idly at the tuft.

At last the ordeal came to an end. The sentry glanced at the east, and appeared to note with satisfaction that his period of duty was coming to an end – as indeed it was, once and for all – for he rubbed his hands and began to walk again briskly to warm himself.

The moment his back was turned the long black snake glided on again, and reached the other thistle tuft, which was within a couple of paces of his return beat.

Back came the sentry and strolled right past the tuft, utterly unconscious of the presence that was crouching behind it. Had he looked down he could scarcely have failed to see, but he did not do so.

He passed, and then his hidden enemy erected himself, and with outstretched hand followed in his tracks.

A moment more, and, just as the Elmoran was about to turn, the great Zulu made a spring, and in the growing light we could see his long lean hands close round the Masai's throat. Then followed a convulsive twining of the two dark bodies, and in another second I saw the Masai's head bent back, and heard a sharp crack, something like that of a dry twig snapping, and he fell down upon the ground, his limbs moving spasmodically.

Umslopogaas had put out all his iron strength and broken the warrior's neck.

For a moment he knelt upon his victim, still gripping his throat till he was sure that there was nothing more to fear from him, and then he rose and beckoned to us to advance, which we did on all fours, like a colony of huge apes. On reaching the kraal we saw that the Masai had still further choked this entrance, which was about ten feet wide – no doubt in order to guard against attack – by dragging four or five tops of mimosa trees up to it. So much the better for us, I reflected; the more obstruction there was the slower would they be able to come through. Here we separated; Mackenzie and his party creeping up under the shadow of the wall to the left, while Sir Henry and Umslopogaas took the stations one on each side of the thorn fence, the two spearmen and the Askari lying down in front of it. I and my men crept on up the right side of the kraal, which was about fifty paces long.

When I was two-thirds up I halted, and placed my men at distances of four paces from one another, keeping Alphonse close to me, however. Then I peeped for the first time over the wall. It was getting fairly light now, and the first thing I saw was the white donkey, exactly opposite to me, and close by it I could make out the pale face of little Flossie, who was sitting as the lad had described, some ten paces from the wall. Round her lay many warriors, sleeping. At distances all over the surface of the kraal were the remains of fires, round each of which slept some five-and-twenty Masai, for the most part gorged with food. Now and then a man would raise himself, yawn, and look at the east, which was turning primrose; but none got up. I determined to wait another five minutes, both to allow the light to increase, so that we could make better shooting, and to give Good and his party – of whom I could see or hear nothing – every opportunity to make ready.

Suddenly, just as I was nerving myself for the signal, having already selected my man on whom I meant to open fire – a great fellow sprawling on the ground within three feet of little Flossie – Alphonse's teeth began to chatter like the hoofs of a galloping giraffe, making a great noise in the silence.

Instantly a Masai within three paces of us woke, and, sitting up, gazed about him, looking for the cause of the sound. Moved beyond myself I brought the butt-end of my rifle down on to the pit of the Frenchman's stomach. This stopped his chattering; but, as he doubled up, he managed to let off his gun in such a manner that the bullet passed within an inch of my head.

There was no need for a signal now. From both sides of the kraal broke out a waving line of fire, in which I myself joined, managing with a snap shot to knock over my Masai by Flossie, just as he was jumping up. Then from the top end of the kraal there rang an awful yell, in which I rejoiced to recognize Good's piercing note rising clear and shrill above the din, and in another second followed such a scene as I have never seen before nor shall again. With an universal howl of terror and fury the brawny crowd of savages within the kraal sprang to their feet, many of them to fall again beneath our well-directed hail of lead before they had moved a yard. For a moment they stood undecided, and then hearing the cries and curses that rose unceasingly from the top end of the kraal, and bewildered by the storm of bullets, they as by one impulse rushed down towards the thorn-stopped entrance. As they went we kept pouring our fire with terrible effect into the thickening mob as fast as we could load. I had emptied my repeater of the ten shots it contained and was just beginning to slip in some more when I bethought me of little Flossie. Looking up, I saw that the white donkey was lying kicking, having been knocked over either by one of our bullets or a Masai spear-thrust. There was no living Masai near, but the black nurse was on her feet and with a spear cutting the rope that bound Flossie's feet. Next second she ran to the wall of the kraal and began to climb over it, an example which the little girl followed. But Flossie was evidently very stiff and cramped, and could only go slowly, and as she went two Masai flying down the kraal caught sight of her and rushed towards her to kill her. The first fellow came up just as the poor little girl, after a desperate effort to climb the wall, fell back into the kraal. Up flashed the great spear, and as it did so a bullet from my rifle found its home in the holder's ribs, and over he went like a shot rabbit. But behind him was the other man, and, alas, I had only that one cartridge in the magazine! Flossie had scrambled to her feet and was facing the second man, who was advancing with raised spear. I turned my head aside and felt sick as death. I could not bear to see him stab her. Glancing up again, to my surprise I saw the Masai's spear lying on the ground, while the man himself was staggering about with both hands to his head. Suddenly I saw a puff of smoke proceeding apparently from Flossie, and the man fell down headlong. Then I remembered the Derringer pistol she carried, and saw that she had fired both barrels of it at him, thereby saving her life. In another instant she had made an effort, and assisted by the nurse, who was lying on the top, had scrambled over the wall, and I knew that she was, comparatively speaking, safe.

By this time some two hundred Masai – allowing that we had up to the present accounted for fifty – had gathered together in front of the thorn-stopped entrance, driven thither by the spears of Good's men, whom they doubtless supposed were a large force instead of being but ten strong. For some reason it never occurred to them to try and rush the wall, which they could have scrambled over with comparative ease; they all made for the fence, which was really a strongly interwoven fortification. With a bound the first warrior went at it, and even before he touched the ground on the other side I saw Sir Henry's great axe swing up and fall with awful force upon his feather head-piece, and he sank into the middle of the thorns. Then with a yell and a crash they began to break through as they might, and ever as they came the great axe swung and Inkosi-kaas flashed and they fell dead one by one, each man thus helping to build up a barrier against his fellows. Those who escaped the axes of the pair fell at the hands of the Askari and the two Mission Kaffirs, and those who passed scatheless from them were brought low by my own and Mackenzie's fire.

Faster and more furious grew the fighting. Single Masai would spring upon the dead bodies of their comrades, and engage one or other of the axemen with their long spears; but, thanks chiefly to the mail shirts, the result was always the same. Presently there was a great swing of the axe, a crashing sound, and another dead Masai. That is, if the man was engaged with Sir Henry. If it was Umslopogaas that he fought with the result indeed would be the same, but it would be differently attained. It was but rarely that the Zulu used the crashing double-handed stroke; on the contrary, he did little more than tap continually at his adversary's head, pecking at it with the pole-axe end of the axe as a woodpecker pecks at rotten wood. Presently a peck would go home, and his enemy would drop down with a neat little circular hole in his forehead or skull, exactly similar to that which a cheese-scoop makes in a cheese.

Good and his men were quite close by now, and our people had to cease firing into the mass for fear of killing some of them (as it was, one of them was slain in this way). Mad and desperate with fear, the Masai by a frantic effort burst through the thorn fence and piled-up dead, and, sweeping Curtis, Umslopogaas, and the other three before them, broke into the open. And now it was that we began to lose men fast. Down went our poor Askari who was armed with the axe, a great spear standing out a foot behind his back; and before long the two spearsmen who had stood with him went down too, dying fighting like tigers; and others of our party shared their fate. For a moment I feared the fight was lost – certainly it trembled in the balance. I shouted to my men to cast down their rifles, and to take spears and throw themselves into the *mêlée*. They obeyed, their blood being now thoroughly up, and Mr Mackenzie's people followed their example.

This move had a momentary good result, but still the fight hung in the balance.

Our people fought magnificently, hurling themselves upon the dark mass of Elmoran, hewing, thrusting, slaying, and being slain. And ever above the din rose Good's awful yell of encouragement as he plunged to wherever the fight was thickest; and ever, with an almost machine-like regularity, the two axes rose and fell, carrying death and disablement at every stroke. But I could see that the strain was beginning to tell upon Sir Henry, who was bleeding from several flesh wounds: his breath was coming in gasps, and the veins stood out on his forehead like blue and knotted cords. Even Umslopogaas, man of iron that he was, was hard pressed. I noticed that he had given up 'woodpecking', and was now using the broad blade of Inkosi-kaas, 'browning' his enemy wherever he could hit him, instead of drilling scientific holes in his head. I myself did not go into the *mêlée*, but hovered outside like the swift 'back' in a football scrimmage, putting a bullet through a Masai whenever I got a chance. I was more use so. I fired forty-nine cartridges that morning, and I did not miss many shots.

Presently, do as we would, the beam of the balance began to rise against us. We had not more than fifteen or sixteen effectives left now, and the Masai had at least fifty. To make matters worse just then, when Mackenzie's rifle was empty, a brawny savage armed with a 'sime', or sword, made a rush for him. The clergyman flung down his gun, and drawing his huge carver from his elastic belt (his revolver had dropped out in the fight), they closed in desperate struggle. Presently, locked in a close embrace, missionary and Masai rolled on to the ground behind the wall, and for some time we remained in ignorance of his fate or how the duel had ended.

To and fro surged the fight, slowly turning round like the vortex of a human whirlpool, and the matter began to look very bad for us. Just then, however, a fortunate thing happened. Umslopogaas, either by accident or design, broke out of the ring and engaged a warrior at some few paces from it. As he did so, another man ran up and struck him with all his force between the shoulders with his great spear, which, falling on the tough steel shirt, failed to pierce it and rebounded. For a moment the man stared aghast – protective armour being unknown among these tribes – and then he yelled out at the top of his voice – '*They are devils – bewitched, bewitched!*' And seized by a sudden panic, he threw down his spear, and began to fly. I cut short his career with a bullet, and Umslopogaas brained his man, and then the panic spread to the others.

'*Bewitched, bewitched!*' they cried, and tried to escape in every direction, utterly demoralized and broken-spirited, for the most part even throwing down their shields and spears. Just as I was hoping that it was all done with, suddenly from under a heap of slain where he had been hiding, an unwounded warrior sprang up, and, clearing the piles of dying and dead like an antelope, sped like the wind up the kraal towards the spot where I was standing at the moment. But he was not alone, for Umslopogaas came gliding on his tracks with the peculiar swallow-like motion for which he was noted, and as they neared me I recognized in the Masai the herald of the previous night. Finding that, run as he would, his pursuer was gaining on him, the man halted and turned round to give battle. Umslopogaas also pulled up.

'Ah, ah,' he cried, in mockery, to the Elmoran, 'it is thou whom I talked with last night – the Lygonani! the Herald! – He who would kill a little girl! And thou didst hope to stand man to man and face to face with Umslopogaas. Behold, thy prayer is granted! And I did swear to hew thee limb from limb, thou insolent dog. Behold, I will do it even now!'

The Masai ground his teeth with fury, and charged at the Zulu with his spear. As he came, Umslopogaas deftly stepped aside, and, swinging Inkosi-kaas high above his head with both hands, brought the broad blade down with such fearful force from behind upon the Masai's shoulder just where the neck is set into the frame, that its razor edge shore right through bone and flesh and muscle, almost severing the head and one arm from the body.

'*Ou!*' ejaculated Umslopogaas, contemplating the corpse of his foe; 'I have kept my word. It was a good stroke.'

EIGHT

The End of the Nightmare

At the kraal entrance the scene was a strange one. The slaughter was over by now, and the wounded men had been put out of their pain, for no quarter had been given. The bush-closed entrance was trampled flat, and in place of bushes it was filled with the bodies of dead men. Dead men, everywhere dead men – they lay about in knots, they were flung by ones and twos in every position upon the open spaces, for all the world like the people on the grass in one of the London parks on a particularly hot Sunday in August. In front of this entrance, on a space which had been cleared of dead and of the shields and spears which were scattered in all directions as they had fallen or been thrown from the hands of their owners, stood and lay the survivors of the awful struggle, and at their feet were four wounded men. We had gone into the fight thirty strong, and of the thirty but fifteen remained alive, and five of them (including Mr Mackenzie) were wounded, two mortally. Of those who held the entrance, Curtis and the Zulu alone remained. Good had lost five men killed, I had lost two killed, and

Mackenzie no less than five out of the six with him. As for the survivors they were, with the exception of myself who had never come to close quarters, red from head to foot – Sir Henry's armour might have been painted that colour – and utterly exhausted, except Umslopogaas, who, as he grimly stood on a little mound above a heap of dead, leaning as usual upon his axe, did not seem particularly distressed, although the skin over the hole in his head palpitated violently.

'Ah, Macumazahn!' he said to me as I limped up, feeling very sick, 'I told thee that it would be a good fight, and it was. Never have I seen a better, or one more bravely fought. As for this iron shirt, surely it is "tagati" (bewitched); nothing could pierce it. Had it not been for the garment I should have been *there*,' and he nodded towards the great pile of dead men beneath him.

'I give it thee; thou art a gallant man,' said Sir Henry, briefly.

Just then Mackenzie asked about Flossie, and we were all greatly relieved when one of the men said he had seen her flying towards the house with the nurse. Then bearing such of the wounded as could be moved at the moment with us, we slowly made our way towards the Mission-house, spent with toil and bloodshed, but with a glorious sense of victory against overwhelming odds glowing in our hearts.

Painfully we made our way up the hill which, but a little more than an hour before, we had descended under such different circumstances. At the gate of the wall stood Mrs Mackenzie waiting for us. When her eyes fell upon us, however, she shrieked out, and covered her face with her hands, crying, 'Horrible, horrible!' Nor were her fears allayed when she discovered her worthy husband being borne upon an improvised stretcher; but her doubts as to the nature of his injury were soon set at rest. Then when in a few brief words I had told her the upshot of the struggle she came up to me and solemnly kissed me on the forehead.

'God bless you all, Mr Quatermain; you have saved my child's life,' she said simply.

Then we went in and got our clothes off and doctored our wounds; I am glad to say I had none, and Sir Henry's and Good's were slight. Mackenzie's, however, was serious, though fortunately the spear had not severed any large artery. After that we had a bath, and what a luxury it was! and having clad ourselves in ordinary clothes, proceeded to the dining-room, where breakfast was set as usual. It was curious sitting down there, drinking tea and eating toast in an ordinary nineteenth-century sort of a way just as though we had not employed the early hours in a regular primitive hand-to-hand middle-ages kind of struggle. As Good said, the whole thing seemed more as though one had had a bad nightmare just before being called, than as a deed done. When we were finishing our breakfast the door opened, and in came little Flossie, very pale and tottery, but quite unhurt. She kissed us all and thanked us. I congratulated her on the presence of mind she had shown in shooting the Masai with her Derringer pistol, and thereby saving her own life.

'Oh, don't talk of it!' she said, beginning to cry hysterically; 'I shall never forget his face as he went turning round and round, never – I can see it now.'

I advised her to go to bed and get some sleep, which she did, and awoke in the evening quite recovered, so far as her strength was concerned.

But poor Flossie! I fear that her nerves will not get over that night in the Masai camp for many a long year.

In the evening I had an interview with Mr Mackenzie, who was suffering a good deal from his wounds, which Good, who was a skilful though unqualified doctor, was treating him for. He told me that this occurrence had taught him a lesson, and that, if he recovered safely, he meant to hand over the Mission to a younger man, who was already on the road to join him in his work, and return to England.

'You see, Quatermain,' he said, 'I made up my mind to it, this very morning, when we were creeping down upon those benighted savages. "If we live through this and rescue Flossie alive," I said to myself, "I will go home to England."'

'I congratulate you on your decision,' answered I, 'for two reasons. The first is, that you owe a duty to your wife and daughter, and more especially to the latter, who should receive some education. The other is, that as sure as I am standing here, sooner or later the Masai will try to avenge the slaughter inflicted on them to-day. Two or three men are sure to have escaped in the confusion who will carry the story back to their people, and the result will be that a great expedition will one day be sent against you. It might be delayed for a year, but sooner or later it will come. Therefore, if only for that reason, I should go. When once they have learnt that you are no longer here they may perhaps leave the place alone.'

'You are quite right,' answered the clergyman. 'I will turn my back upon this place in a month. But it will be a wrench, it will be a wrench.'

NINE
Into The Unknown

A week had passed, and we all sat at supper one night in the Mission dining-room, feeling very much depressed in spirits, for the reason that we were going to say good-bye to our kind friends, the Mackenzies, and depart upon our way at dawn on the morrow.

Whilst we were sitting on the verandah, smoking a pipe before turning in, who should come up to us but Alphonse, and, with a magnificent bow, announce his wish for an interview. Being requested to 'fire away', he explained at some length that he was anxious to attach himself to our party – a statement that astonished me not a little. The reason, however, soon appeared. Mr Mackenzie was going down to the coast, and thence on to England. Now, if he went down country, Alphonse was persuaded that he would be seized, extradited, sent to France, and to penal servitude.

After listening to what he had to say, we consulted among ourselves, and finally agreed, with Mr Mackenzie's knowledge and consent, to accept his offer. To begin with, we were very short-handed, and Alphonse was a quick, active fellow, who could turn his hand to anything, and cook – ah, he *could* cook!

So, after warning him of the undoubted risks he was exposing himself to, we told him that we would accept his offer on condition that he would promise implicit obedience to our orders. We also promised to give him wages at the rate of ten pounds a month should he ever return to a civilized country to receive them. To all of this he agreed with alacrity, and retired to write a letter to his Annette, which Mr Mackenzie promised to post when he got down country.

Well, the morrow came, and by seven o'clock the donkeys were all loaded, and the time of parting was at hand. It was a melancholy business, especially saying good-bye to dear little Flossie.

After leaving the Mission-house we made our way, comparatively unmolested, past the base of Mt Kenia, which the Masai call 'Donyo Egere', or the 'speckled mountain', on account of the black patches of rock that appear upon its mighty spire, where the sides are too precipitous to allow of the snow lying on them; then on past the lonely lake Baringo, where one of our two remaining Askari, having unfortunately trodden upon a puff-adder, died of snake-bite, in spite of all our efforts to save him. Thence we proceeded a distance of about a hundred and fifty miles to another magnificent snow-clad mountain called Lekakisera. There we rested a fortnight, and then started out into the trackless and uninhabited forest of a vast district called Elgumi. On emerging from the great Elgumi forest, we, still steering northwards, in accordance with the information Mr Mackenzie had collected from the unfortunate wanderer struck the base in due course of the large lake, called Laga by the natives, which is about fifty miles long by twenty broad, and of which, it may be remembered, he made mention. Thence we pushed on nearly a month's journey over great rolling uplands, something like those in the Transvaal, but diversified by patches of bush country.

All this time we were continually ascending at the rate of about one hundred feet every ten miles. Indeed the country was on a slope which appeared to terminate at a mass of snow-tipped mountains, for which we were steering, and where we learnt the second lake of which the wanderer had spoken as the lake without a bottom was situated. At length we arrived there, and, having ascertained that there *was* a large lake on the top of the mountains, ascended three thousand feet more till we came to a precipitous cliff or edge, to find a great sheet of water some twenty miles square lying fifteen hundred feet below us, and evidently occupying an extinct volcanic crater or craters of vast extent. Perceiving villages on the border of this lake, we descended with great difficulty through forests of pine-trees, which now clothed the precipitous sides of the crater, and were well received by the people, a simple, unwarlike folk, who had never seen or even heard of a white man before, and treated us with great reverence and kindness, supplying us with as much food and milk as we could eat and drink. This wonderful and beautiful lake lay, according to our aneroid, at a height of no less than 11,450 feet above sea-level, and its climate was quite cold, and not at all unlike that of England. There we purchased a capital log canoe, and we set out to make a tour of the lake in order to find the most favourable place to make a camp. As we did not know if we should return to this village, we put all our gear into the canoe, and also a quarter of cooked water-buck, which when young is delicious eating, and off we set, natives having already gone before us in light canoes to warn the inhabitants of the other villages of our approach.

As we were paddling leisurely along Good remarked upon the extraordinary deep blue colour of the water, and

said that he understood from the natives, who were great
fishermen – fish, indeed, being their principal food – that
the lake was supposed to be wonderfully deep, and to have a
hole at the bottom through which the water escaped and put
out some great fire that was raging below.

The farther shore of the lake we found, on approaching
it, to consist of a vast perpendicular wall of rock, which held
the water without any intermediate sloping bank, as elsewhere. Accordingly we paddled parallel with this precipice,
at a distance of about a hundred paces from it, shaping our
course for the end of the lake, where we knew that there was
a large village.

As we went we began to pass a considerable accumulation
of floating rushes, weed, boughs of trees, and other rubbish, brought, Good supposed, to this spot by some current, which he was much puzzled to account for. Whilst we
were speculating about this, Sir Henry pointed out a flock of
large white swans, which were feeding on the drift some
little way ahead of us. Now I had already noticed swans
flying about this lake, and, having never come across them
before in Africa, was exceedingly anxious to obtain a specimen. I had questioned the natives about them, and learnt
that they came from over the mountain, always arriving at
certain periods of the year in the early morning, when it was
very easy to catch them, on account of their exhausted
condition.

Well, we set to work to stalk the swans, which kept
drawing, as they fed, nearer and nearer to the precipice, and
at last we pushed the canoe under shelter of a patch of drift
within forty yards of them. Sir Henry had the shot-gun,
loaded and, waiting for a chance, got two in a line, and,
firing at their necks, killed them both. Up rose the rest,
thirty or more of them, with a mighty splashing; and, as
they did so, he gave them the other barrel. Down came one
fellow with a broken wing, and I saw the leg of another drop

and a few feathers start out of his back; but he went on quite strong.

We picked up our two dead ones, and beautiful birds they were, weighing not less than about thirty pounds each, and were chasing the winged one, which had scrambled over a mass of driftweed into a pool of clear water beyond. Finding a difficulty in forcing the canoe through the rubbish, I told our only remaining Wakwafi servant, whom I knew to be an excellent swimmer, to jump over, dive under the drift, and catch him, knowing that as there were no crocodiles in this lake he could come to no harm. Entering into the fun of the thing, the man obeyed, and soon was dodging about after the winged swan in fine style, getting gradually nearer to the rock wall, against which the water washed as he did so.

Presently he gave up swimming after the swan, and began to cry out that he was being carried away; and, indeed, we saw that, though he was swimming with all his strength towards us, he was being drawn slowly towards the precipice. With a few desperate strokes of our paddles we pushed the canoe through the crust of drift and rowed towards the man as hard as we could, but, fast as we went, he was drawn faster towards the rock. Suddenly I saw that before us, just rising eighteen inches or so above the surface of the lake, was what looked like the top of the arch of a submerged cave or railway tunnel. Evidently, from the watermark on the rock several feet above it, it was generally entirely submerged; but there had been a dry season, and the cold had prevented the snow from melting as freely as usual; so the lake was low and the arch showed. Towards this arch our poor servant was being sucked with frightful rapidity. He was not more than ten fathoms from it, and we were about twenty when I saw it, and with little help from us the canoe flew along after him. He struggled bravely, and I thought that we should have saved him, when suddenly I perceived an expression of despair come upon his face, and there before our eyes he was sucked down into the cruel swirling blue depths, and vanished. At the same moment I felt our canoe seized as with a mighty hand, and propelled with resistless force towards the rock.

We realized our danger now and rowed, or rather paddled, furiously in our attempt to get out of the vortex. In vain; in another second we were flying straight for the arch like an arrow, and I thought that we were lost. Luckily I retained sufficient presence of mind to shout out, instantly setting the example by throwing myself into the bottom of the canoe, 'Down on your faces – down!' and the others had the sense to take the hint. In another instant there was a grinding noise, and the boat was pushed down till the water began to trickle over the sides, and I thought that we were gone. But no, suddenly the grinding ceased, and we could again feel the canoe flying alone. I turned my head a little – I dared not lift it – and looked up. By the feeble light that yet reached the canoe, I could make out that a dense arch of rock hung just over our heads, and that was all. In another minute I could not even see as much as that, for the faint light had merged into shadow, and the shadows had been swallowed up in darkness, utter and complete.

For an hour or so we lay there, not daring to lift our heads for fear lest the brains should be dashed out of them, and scarcely able to speak even, on account of the noise of the rushing water which drowned our voices. Not, indeed, that we had much inclination to speak, seeing that we were overwhelmed by the awfulness of our position and the imminent fear of instant death, either by being dashed against the sides of the cavern, or on a rock, or being sucked down in the raging waters, or perhaps asphyxiated by want of air. All of these and many other modes of death presented themselves to my imagination as I lay at the bottom of the canoe, listening to the swirl of the hurrying waters which ran whither we knew not.

TEN
The Rose of Fire

On we flew, drawn by the mighty current, till at last I noticed that the sound of the water was not half so deafening as it had been, and concluded that this must be because there was more room for the echoes to disperse in. Cautiously I raised myself on my knees and stretched my hand upwards, but could touch no roof. Next I took the paddle and lifted it above my head as high as I could, but with the same result. I also thrust it out laterally to the right and left, but could touch nothing except water. Then I bethought me that there was in the boat, amongst our other remaining possessions, a bull's-eye lantern and a tin of oil. I groped about and found it, and having a match on me carefully lit it, and as soon as the flame had got a hold of the wick I turned it on down the boat. Good was lying on the flat of his back, his eyeglass still fixed in his eye, and gazing blankly into the upper darkness. Sir Henry had his head resting on the thwarts of the canoe, and with his hand was trying to test the speed of the water.

We began to discuss the situation as well as we could.

First, however, at Good's suggestion, we bound two paddles mast-fashion in the bows so that they might give us warning against any sudden lowering of the roof of the cave or waterway. It was clear to us that we were in an underground river which carried off the superfluous waters of the lake. That the river was wide we could clearly see, for the light from the bull's-eye lantern failed to reach from shore to shore, although occasionally, when the current swept us either to one side or the other, we could distinguish the rock wall of the tunnel, which, as far as we could make out, appeared to arch about twenty-five feet above our heads. As for the current itself, it ran, Good estimated, at least eight knots, and, fortunately for us, was, as is usual, fiercest in the middle of the stream. Still, our first act was to arrange that one of us, with the lantern and a pole there was in the canoe, should always be in the bows ready, if possible, to prevent us from being stove in against the side of the cave or any projecting rock. Umslopogaas took the first turn. This was absolutely, with one exception, all that we could do towards preserving our safety. The exception was that another of us took up a position in the stern with a paddle by means of which it was possible to steer the canoe more or less and to keep her from the sides of the cave. These matters attended to, we made a somewhat sparing meal off the cold buck's meat (for we did not know how long it might have to last us), and then feeling in rather better spirits I gave my opinion that, serious as it undoubtedly was, I did not consider our position altogether without hope, unless, indeed, the natives were right, and the river plunged straight down into the bowels of the earth. If not, it was clear that it must emerge somewhere, probably on the other side of the mountains, and in that case all we had to think of was to keep ourselves alive till we got there, wherever 'there' might be.

'Well, let us hope for the best and prepare ourselves for

the worst,' said Sir Henry, who is always cheerful and even spirited – a very tower of strength in the time of trouble.

This was excellent advice, and we proceeded to take it each in our separate way. Good was at the helm and Umslopogaas in the bows, so there was nothing left for Sir Henry and myself to do except to lie down in the canoe and think. It certainly was a curious, and indeed almost a weird, position to be placed in – rushing along, as we were, through the bowels of the earth. And how dark it was! the feeble ray from our little lamp did but serve to show the darkness. There in the bows sat old Umslopogaas, watchful and untiring, the pole ready to his hand, and behind in the shadow I could just make out the form of Good peering forward at the ray of light in order to make out how to steer with the paddle that he held and now and again dipped in the water.

It was nearly midday when we made our dive into darkness, and we had set our watch (Good and Umslopogaas) at two, having agreed that it should be of a duration of five hours. At seven o'clock, accordingly, Sir Henry and I went on, Sir Henry at the bow and I at the stern, and the other two lay down and went to sleep. For three hours all went well, Sir Henry only finding it necessary once to push us off from the side; and I that but little steering was required to keep us straight, as the violent current did all that was needed, though occasionally the canoe showed a tendency which had to be guarded against to veer and travel broadside on.

When I had been for three hours or so at the helm, I began to notice a decided change in the temperature, which was getting warmer. At first I took no notice of it, but when, at the expiration of another half-hour, I found that it was getting hotter and hotter, I called to Sir Henry and asked him if he noticed it, or if it was only my imagination. 'Noticed it!' he answered; 'I should think so. I am in a sort of Turkish bath.' Just about then the others woke up gasping, and were obliged to begin to discard their clothes. Here Umslopogaas had the advantage, for he did not wear any to speak of, except a moocha.

Hotter it grew, and hotter yet, till at last we could scarcely breathe, and the perspiration poured out of us. Half an hour more, and though we were all now stark naked, we could hardly bear it. I dipped my hand into the water and drew it out almost with a cry; it was nearly boiling. We consulted a little thermometer we had – the mercury stood at 123°. From the surface of the water rose a dense cloud of steam.

Our sufferings for some time after this really pass my powers of description. We no longer perspired, for all the perspiration had been sweated out of us. We simply lay in the bottom of the boat, which we were now physically incapable of directing, feeling like hot embers. Our skins began to crack, and the blood to throb in our heads like the beating of a steam-engine.

This had been going on for some time, when suddenly the river turned a little, and I heard Sir Henry call out from the bows in a hoarse, startled voice, and, looking up, saw a most wonderful and awful thing. About half a mile ahead of us a huge pillar-like jet of almost white flame rose from the surface of the water and sprang fifty feet into the air, when it struck the roof and spread out some forty feet in diameter, falling back in curved sheets of fire shaped like the petals of a full-blown rose. Indeed this awful gas jet resembled nothing so much as a great flaming flower rising out of the black water. It lit up the whole cavern as clear as day, and we could see that the roof was here about forty feet above us, and washed perfectly smooth with water. On we rushed towards this pillar of fire, which gleamed fiercer than any furnace ever lit by man.

'Keep the boat to the right, Quatermain – to the right,' shouted Sir Henry, and a minute afterwards I saw him fall forward senseless. Alphonse had already gone. Good was the next to go. There they lay as though dead: only Umslopogaas and I kept our senses. We were within fifty yards of it now, and I saw the Zulu's head fall forward on his hands. He had gone too, and I was alone. I could not breathe; the fierce heat dried me up. For yards and yards round the great rose of fire the rock-roof was red-hot. The wood of the boat was almost burning. I saw the feathers on one of the dead swans begin to twist and shrivel up; but I would not give in. I knew that if I did we should pass within three or four yards of the gas jet and perish miserably. I set the paddle so as to turn the canoe as far from it as possible and held on grimly.

My eyes seemed to be bursting from my head, and through my closed lids I could see the fierce light. We were nearly opposite now; it roared like all the fires of hell, and the water boiled furiously around it. Five seconds more. We were past; I heard the roar behind me.

Then I too fell senseless. The next thing that I recollect is feeling a breath of air upon my face. My eyes opened with great difficulty. I looked up. Far, far above me there was light, though around me was deep gloom. Then I remembered and looked. The canoe still floated down the river, and in the bottom of it lay the naked forms of my companions. 'Were they dead?' I wondered. 'Was I left alone in this awful place?' I knew not. Next I became conscious of a burning thirst. I put my hand over the edge of the boat into the water and drew it up again with a cry. No wonder: nearly all the skin was burnt off the back of it. The water, however, was cold, or nearly so, and I drank pints and splashed myself all over. My body seemed to suck up the fluid as one may see a brick wall suck up rain after a drought; but where I was burnt the touch of it caused intense pain. Then I bethought myself of the others, and, dragging myself towards them with difficulty, I sprinkled

them with water, and to my joy they began to recover –
Umslopogaas first, then the others. Next they drank,
absorbing water like so many sponges. Then, feeling chilly
– a queer contrast to our recent sensations – we began as best
we could to get into our clothes. As we did so Good pointed
to the port side of the canoe: it was all blistered with heat,
and in places actually charred.

As soon as we had got some things on and shaken
ourselves together a little, we set to work to make out where
we were now. I have said that there was light above, and on
examination we found that it came from the sky. Our river
was no longer underground but was running on its dark-
some way, between two frightful cliffs which cannot have
been less than two thousand feet high. So high were they,
indeed, that though the sky was above us, where we were
was dense gloom – not darkness indeed, but the gloom of
a room closely shuttered in the daytime. Up on either
side rose the great straight cliffs, grim and forbidding,
till the eye grew dizzy with trying to measure their sheer
height.

By the river's edge was a little shore formed of round
fragments of rock washed into this shape by the constant
action of water, and giving the place the appearance of being
strewn with thousands of fossil cannon balls. And here, on
this beach, we determined to land, in order to rest ourselves
a little after all that we had gone through and to stretch our
limbs. It was a dreadful place, but it would give an hour's
respite from the terrors of the river, and also allow of our
repacking and arranging the canoe. Accordingly we
selected what looked like a favourable spot, and with some
little difficulty managed to beach the canoe and scramble
out on to the round, inhospitable pebbles.

'My word,' called out Good, who was on shore the first,
'what an awful place! it's enough to give one a fit.' And he
laughed in a rather hysterical way.

Instantly a thundering voice took up his words, magnifying them a hundred times. '*Give one a fit – Ho! ho! ho!*' – '*A fit! Ho! ho! ho!*' answered another voice in wild accents from far up the cliff – *a fit! a fit! a fit!* chimed in voice after voice – each flinging the words to and fro with shouts of awful laughter to the invisible lips of the other till the whole place echoed with the words and with shrieks of fiendish merriment, which at last ceased as suddenly as they had begun.

'Oh, mon Dieu!' yelled Alphonse, startled quite out of such self-command as he possessed.

'*Mon Dieu! Mon Dieu! Mon Dieu!*' the Titanic echoes thundered, shrieked, and wailed in every conceivable tone.

After this we found it necessary to keep our conversation down to a whisper – for it was really unbearable to have every word one uttered tossed to and fro like a tennis-ball, as precipice called to precipice.

But even our whispers ran up the rocks in mysterious murmurs till at last they died away in long-drawn sighs of sound. Echoes are delightful and romantic things, but we had more than enough of them in that dreadful gulf.

As soon as we had settled ourselves a little on the round stones, we went on to wash and dress our burns as well as we could. Then we repacked the canoe, and finally began to take some food, of which I need scarcely say we were in need, for our insensibility had endured for many hours, and it was, as our watches showed, midday.

The gloom was so intense that we could scarcely see the way to cut our food and convey it to our mouths. Still we got on pretty well till I happened to look behind me – my attention being attracted by a noise of something crawling over the stones, and perceived sitting upon a rock in my immediate rear a huge species of black freshwater crab, only it was five times the size of any crab I ever saw. This hideous and loathsome-looking animal had projecting eyes that seemed to glare at one, very long and flexible antennæ or

feelers, and gigantic claws. Nor was I especially favoured
with its company. From every quarter dozens of these
horrid brutes were creeping up, drawn, I suppose, by the
smell of the food, from between the round stones and out of
holes in the precipice. Some were already quite close to us. I
stared quite fascinated by the unusual sight, and as I did so I
saw one of the beasts stretch out its huge claw and give the
unsuspecting Good such a nip behind that he jumped up
with a howl, and set the 'wild echoes flying' in sober earnest.
Just then, too, another, a very large one, got hold of
Alphonse's leg, and declined to part with it, and, as may be
imagined, a considerable scene ensued. Umslopogaas took
his axe and cracked the shell of one with the flat of it,
whereon it set up a horrid screaming which the echoes
multiplied a thousandfold, and began to foam at the mouth,
a proceeding that drew hundreds more of its friends out of
unsuspected holes and corners. Those on the spot perceiving that the animal was hurt fell upon it like creditors on a
bankrupt, and literally rent it limb from limb with their
huge pincers and devoured it, using their claws to convey
the fragments to their mouths. Seizing whatever weapons
were handy, such as stones or paddles, we commenced a
war upon the monsters – whose numbers were increasing by
leaps and bounds, and whose stench was overpowering. So
fast as we cracked their armour others seized the injured
ones and devoured them, foaming at the mouth, and
screaming as they did so. Nor did the brutes stop at that.
When they could they nipped hold of us – and awful nips
they were – or tried to steal the meat. One enormous fellow
got hold of the swan we had skinned and began to drag it off.
Instantly a score of others flung themselves upon the prey,
and then began a ghastly and disgusting scene. How the
monsters foamed and screamed, and rent the flesh, and each
other! It was a sickening and unnatural sight, and one that
will haunt all who saw it till their dying day – enacted as it

was in the deep, oppressive gloom, and set to the unceasing music of the many-toned nerve-shaking echoes.

'I say, you fellows, let's get out of this or we shall all go off our heads,' sung out Good; and we were not slow to take the hint. Pushing the canoe, around which the animals were now crawling by hundreds and making vain attempts to climb, off the rocks, we bundled into it and got out into mid-stream, leaving behind us the fragments of our meal and the screaming, foaming, stinking mass of monsters in full possession of the ground.

'What's to be done next?' said Sir Henry blankly.

'Drift, I suppose,' I answered, and we drifted accordingly. All the afternoon and well into the evening we floated on in the gloom beneath the far-off line of blue sky, scarcely knowing when day ended and night began, for down in that vast gulf the difference was not marked, till at length Good pointed out a star hanging right above us, which, having nothing better to do, we observed with great interest. Suddenly it vanished, the darkness became intense, and a familiar murmuring sound filled the air. 'Underground again,' I said with a groan, holding up the lamp. Yes, there was no doubt about it. I could just make out the roof. The chasm had come to an end and the tunnel had recommenced. And so the hours passed till it was nearly three o'clock. Sir Henry, Good, and Alphonse were asleep, utterly worn out; Umslopogaas was at the bow with the pole, and I was steering, when I perceived that the rate at which we were travelling had perceptibly increased. Then, suddenly, I heard Umslopogaas make an exclamation, and next second came a sound as of parting branches, and I became aware that the canoe was being forced through hanging bushes or creepers. Another minute, and a breath of sweet open air fanned my face, and I felt that we had emerged from the tunnel and were floating upon clear water. I say felt, for I could see nothing, the darkness being absolutely pitchy, as it often is just before the dawn. But even this could scarcely damp my joy. We were out of that dreadful river, and wherever we might have got to this at least was something to be thankful for. And so I sat down and inhaled the sweet night air and waited for the dawn with such patience as I could command.

ELEVEN

The Frowning City

For an hour or more I sat waiting (Umslopogaas having meanwhile gone to sleep also) till at length the east turned grey, and day dawned.

But as yet I could see nothing save the beautiful blue sky above, for over the water was a thick layer of mist exactly as though the whole surface had been covered with billows of cotton wool. By degrees, however, the sun sucked up the mists, and then I saw that we were afloat upon a glorious sheet of blue water of which I could not make out the shore. Some eight or ten miles behind us, however, there stretched as far as the eye could reach a range of precipitous hills that formed a retaining wall of the lake. Presently Umslopogaas called my attention to a whitish object upon the water and with a few strokes of the paddle brought the canoe to the spot, whereupon we discovered that the object was the body of a man floating face downwards. This was bad enough, but imagine my horror when Umslopogaas having turned him on to his back with the paddle, we recognized in the sunken features the lineaments of our poor servant who had been sucked down two days before in the waters of the subterranean river. It quite frightened me. I thought that we had left him behind for ever, and behold! borne by the current, he had made the awful journey with us, and with us had reached the end. His appearance also was dreadful, for he bore traces of having touched the pillar of fire – one arm being completely shrivelled up and all his hair being burnt off. The features were, as I have said, sunken, and yet they preserved upon them that awful look of despair that I had seen upon his living face as the poor fellow was sucked down. Really the sight unnerved me, weary and shaken as I felt with all that we had gone through, and I was heartily glad when suddenly and without any warning the body began to sink just as though it had had a mission, which having been accomplished, it retired.

Down it went into the transparent depths – fathom after fathom we could trace its course till at last a long line of bright air-bubbles, swiftly chasing each other to the surface, alone remained where it had passed. At length these, too, were gone, and that was an end of our poor servant. Umslopogaas thoughtfully watched the body vanish.

'What did he follow us for?' he asked. ''Tis an ill omen for thee and me, Macumazahn.' And he laughed grimly.

Just then, the others woke up and began to rejoice exceedingly at finding that we were out of that dreadful river and once more beneath the blue sky. Then Good began to search the horizon with the spy-glass, and suddenly announced joyfully that he saw land, and pointed out that, from the change in the colour of the water, he thought we must be approaching the mouth of a river. In another minute we perceived a great golden dome, not unlike that of St Paul's, piercing the morning mists, and while we were wondering what in the world it could be, Good reported another and still more important discovery, namely, that a small sailing-boat was advancing towards us carrying a singularly large sail for her size. But our attention was soon diverted from the boat to her crew, which consisted of a man and woman, *nearly as white as ourselves*.

We stared at each other in amazement, thinking that we must be mistaken; but no, there was no doubt about it.

So it was true, after all; and, mysteriously led by a Power beyond our own, we had discovered this wonderful people. I could have shouted for joy when I thought of the glory and the wonder of the thing; and as it was, we all shook hands and congratulated each other on the unexpected success of our wild search.

Meanwhile, if we had been astonished at the appearance of the man and woman, it was clear that they were far more astonished at us. As for the man, he appeared to be overcome with fear and wonder, and for a while hovered round our canoe, but would not approach. At last, however, he came within hailing distance, and called to us in a language that sounded soft and pleasing enough, but of which we could not understand one word. So we hailed back in English, French, Latin, Greek, German, Zulu, Dutch, Sisutu, Kukuana, and a few other native dialects that I am acquainted with, but our visitor did not understand any of these tongues; indeed, they appeared to bewilder him.

At length, the man, being unable to make anything out of us, suddenly headed his boat round and began to head off for the shore, his little boat skimming away before the wind like a swallow.

'It is very clear to me,' I said, 'that the man will be back before long with a host of his fellows, so we had best make up our minds as to how we are going to receive them.'

'But how will they receive us?' said Sir Henry.

As for Good he made no remark, but began to extract a small square tin case that had accompanied us in all our wanderings from under a pile of baggage. Now we had often remonstrated with Good about this tin case, inasmuch as it had been an awkward thing to carry, and he had never given any very explicit account as to its contents; but he had insisted on keeping it, saying mysteriously that it might come in very useful one day.

'What on earth are you going to do, Good?' asked Sir Henry.

'Do – why dress, of course! You don't expect me to appear in a new country in these things, do you?' and he pointed to his soiled and worn garments, which were however, like all Good's things, very tidy, and with every tear neatly mended.

We said no more, but watched his proceedings with breathless interest. His first step was to get Alphonse, who was thoroughly competent in such matters, to trim his hair and beard in the most approved fashion. I think that if he had had some hot water and cake of soap at hand he would have shaved off the latter; but he had not. This done, he suggested that we should lower the sail of the canoe and all take a bath, which we did, greatly to the horror and astonishment of Alphonse, who lifted his hands and ejaculated that these English were indeed a wonderful people. Umslopogaas, who, though he was, like most high-bred Zulus, scrupulously cleanly in his person, did not see the fun of swimming about in a lake, also regarded the proceeding with mild amusement. We got back into the canoe much refreshed by the cold water, and sat to dry in the sun, whilst Good undid his tin box, and produced first a beautiful clean white shirt, just as it had left a London steam laundry, and then some garments wrapped first in brown, then in white, and finally in silver paper. We watched this undoing with the tenderest interest and much speculation. One by one Good removed the dull husks that hid their splendours, carefully folding and replacing each piece of paper as he did so; and there at last lay, in all the majesty of its gold epaulettes, lace, and buttons, a Commander of the Royal

Navy's full-dress uniform – dress sword, cocked hat, shiny patent leather boots and all. We literally gasped.

'*What!*' we said, '*what!* Are you going to put those things on?'

'Certainly,' he answered composedly; 'you see so much depends upon a first impression, especially,' he added, 'as I observe that there are ladies about. One at least of us ought to be decently dressed.'

When at last he stood up in all his glory, even down to the medals on his breast, and contemplated himself in the still waters of the lake, after the fashion of the young gentleman in ancient history, whose name I cannot remember, but who fell in love with his own shadow, Umslopogaas could no longer restrain his feelings.

'Oh, Bougwan!' he said. 'Oh, Bougwan! I always thought thee an ugly little man, and fat – fat as the cows at calving time; and now thou art like a blue jay when he spreads his tail out. Surely, Bougwan, it hurts my eyes to look at thee.'

Good did not much like this allusion to his fat. But on the whole he was pleased at Umslopogaas's admiration.

As we gazed upon the beauties thus revealed by Good, a spirit of emulation filled our breasts, and we set to work to get ourselves up as well as we could. The most, however, that we were able to do was to array ourselves in our spare suits of shooting clothes, of which we each had one, keeping on our mail shirts underneath.

All this while, having hoisted the sail again as soon as we had finished bathing, we had been progressing steadily for the land, or, rather, for the mouth of a great river. Presently – in all about an hour and a half after the little boat had left us – we saw emerging from the river or harbour a large number of boats, ranging up to ten or twelve tons burden. One of these was propelled by twenty-four oars, and most of the rest sailed. Looking through the glass we soon made out that the row-boat was an official vessel, her crew being all dressed in a sort of uniform, whilst on the half-deck forward stood an old man of venerable appearance, and with a flowing white beard, and a sword strapped to his side, who was evidently the commander of the craft. The other boats were apparently occupied by people brought out by curiosity, and were rowing or sailing towards us as quickly as they could.

Just then Good spied a school of hippopotami on the water about two hundred yards off us, and suggested that it would not be a bad plan to impress the natives with a sense of our power by shooting some of them if possible. This, unluckily enough, struck us as a good idea, and accordingly we at once got out our eight-bore rifles, for which we still had a few cartridges left, and prepared for action.

On glancing up, I perceived that the people we had fallen among were evidently ignorant of the nature of firearms, for the consternation caused by our shots and their effect upon the animals was prodigious. Some of the parties in the boats began to cry out with fear; others turned and made off as hard as they could; and even the old gentleman with the sword looked greatly puzzled and alarmed, and halted his big row-boat.

The boats had gathered together at a distance, and we could see that their occupants, who were evidently much frightened, were consulting what to do. Without giving them time for further consideration, which we thought might result unfavourably to ourselves, we instantly took our paddles and advanced towards them, Good standing in the bow and taking off his cocked hat politely in every direction, his amiable features suffused by a bland but intelligent smile. Most of the craft retreated as we advanced, but a few held their ground, while the big row-boat came on to meet us. Presently we were alongside, and I could see that our appearance – and especially Good's and

Umslopogaas's – filled the venerable-looking commander
with astonishment, not unmixed with awe.

Good took off his hat to the old gentleman with an extra
flourish, and inquired after his health in the purest English,
to which he replied by laying the first two fingers of his right
hand horizontally across his lips and holding them there for
a moment, which we took as his method of salutation. Then
we came to a standstill, till I, being exceedingly hungry,
thought I might as well call attention to the fact, and did so
first by opening my mouth and pointing down it, and then
rubbing my stomach. These signals the old gentleman
clearly understood, for he nodded his head vigorously, and
pointed towards the harbour; and at the same time one of
the men on his boat threw us a line and motioned to us to
make it fast, which we did. The row-boat then took us in
tow, and went with great rapidity towards the mouth of the
river, accompanied by all the other boats. In about twenty
minutes more we reached the entrance to the harbour,
which was crowded with boats full of people who had come
out to see us. Presently the wide river gave a sweep, and
when it did so an exclamation of astonishment and delight
burst from our lips as we caught our first view of the place
that we afterwards knew as Milosis, or the Frowning City
(from *mi*, which means city, and *losis*, a frown).

At a distance of some five hundred yards from the river's
bank rose a sheer precipice of granite, two hundred feet or
so in height. On the brow of this precipice stood a great
building of the same granite that formed the cliff, built on
three sides of a square, the fourth side being open, save for a
kind of battlement pierced at its base by a little door. This
imposing place we afterwards discovered was the palace of
the queen, or rather of the queens. At the back of the palace
the town sloped gently upwards to a flashing building of
white marble, crowned by the golden dome which we had
already observed. Right in front of us was the wonder and

glory of Milosis – the great staircase of the palace, the magnificence of which fairly took our breath away. Let the reader imagine a splendid stairway, sixty-five feet from balustrade to balustrade, consisting of two vast flights, each of one hundred and twenty-five steps of eight inches in height by three feet broad, connected by a flat resting-place sixty feet in length, and running from the palace wall on the edge of the precipice down to meet a waterway or canal to its foot from the river. This marvellous staircase was supported upon a single enormous granite arch, of which the resting-place between the two flights formed the crown; that is, the connecting open space lay upon it.

This staircase with its supports was, indeed, a work of which any living man might have been proud, both on account of its magnitude and its surpassing beauty. Four times, as we afterwards learnt, did the work, which was commenced in remote antiquity, fail, and was then abandoned for three centuries when half-finished, till at last there rose a youthful engineer named Rademas, who said that he would complete it successfully, and staked his life upon it. If he failed he was to be hurled from the precipice he had undertaken to scale; if he succeeded, he was to be rewarded by the hand of the king's daughter. Five years was given to him to complete the work, and an unlimited supply of labour and material. Three times did his arch fall, till at last, seeing failure to be inevitable, he determined to commit suicide on the morrow of the third collapse. That night, however, a beautiful woman came to him in a dream and touched his forehead, and of a sudden he saw a vision of the completed work, and saw too through the masonry and how the difficulties that had hitherto baffled his genius were to be overcome. Then he woke and once more commenced the work, but on a different plan, and behold! he achieved it, and on the last day of the five years he led the princess his bride up the stair and into the palace. And in due course he became king by right of his wife, and founded the present Zu-Vendi dynasty, which is to this day called the 'House of the Stairway'. And to commemorate his triumph he fashioned a statue of himself dreaming, and of the fair woman who touched him on the forehead, and placed it in the great hall of the palace, and there it stands to this day.

TWELVE

The Sister Queens

The big rowing-boat glided on up the cutting that ran almost to the foot of the vast stairway, and then halted at a flight of steps leading to the landing-place. Here the old gentleman disembarked, and invited us to do so likewise.

As soon as we were on shore, a number of the men who had rowed the big boat took possession of our few goods and chattels, and started with them up the splendid staircase, our guide indicating to us by means of motions that the things were perfectly safe. This done, he turned to the right and led the way to a small house, which was, as I afterwards discovered, an inn. Entering into a good-sized room, we saw that a wooden table was already furnished with food, presumably in preparation for us. Here our guide motioned us to be seated on a bench that ran the length of the table. We did not require a second invitation, but at once fell to ravenously on the viands before us, which were served on wooden platters, and consisted of cold goat's flesh, wrapped up in some kind of leaf that gave it a delicious flavour, green vegetables resembling lettuces, brown bread, and red wine

poured from a skin into horn mugs. This wine was peculiarly soft and good, having something of the flavour of
Burgundy. Twenty minutes after we sat down at that
hospitable board we rose from it, feeling like new men.
After all that we had gone through we needed two things,
food and rest, and the food of itself was a great blessing to
us.

As soon as we had finished our meal, our venerable conduc-
tor, who had been standing all the while, regarding us with
inquiring eyes, and our guns with something as like fear as
his pride would allow him to show, bowed towards Good,
whom he evidently took for the leader of the party on
account of the splendour of his apparel, and once more led
the way through the door and to the foot of the great
staircase.

On we went up the first flight of one hundred and twenty
steps, across the broad platform joining it to the second
flight. Then we passed on up the stair till at last we reached
the top, where we found a large standing space to which
there were three entrances, all of small size. Two of these
opened on to rather narrow galleries or roadways cut in the
face of the precipice that ran round the palace walls and led
to the principal thoroughfares of the city, and were used by
the inhabitants passing up and down from the docks. These
were defended by gates of bronze. The third entrance
consisted of a flight of ten curved black marble steps leading
to a doorway cut in the palace wall. This wall was in itself a
work of art, being built of huge blocks of granite to the
height of forty feet, and so fashioned that its face was
concave, whereby it was rendered practically impossible for
it to be scaled. To this doorway our guide led us. The door,
which was very massive, and made of wood protected by an
outer gate of bronze, was closed; but on our approach it was
thrown wide, and we were met by the challenge of a sentry,
who was armed with a heavy triangular-bladed spear, not

unlike a bayonet in shape, and a cutting sword, and protected by breast and back plates of skilfully prepared hippopotamus hide, and a small round shield fashioned of the same tough material. The sword instantly attracted our attention; it was practically identical with the one in the possession of Mr Mackenzie which he had obtained from the ill-starred wanderer. Our guide instantly gave a password, which the soldier acknowledged by letting the iron shaft of his spear fall with a ringing sound upon the pavement, and we passed on. Finally, we came to the great hall of the palace, and once more stood astonished at the simple and yet overpowering grandeur of the place.

In the exact centre of the hall was a solid mass of black marble about the size of a baby's arm-chair, which it rather resembled in appearance. This, as we afterwards learnt, was the sacred stone of this remarkable people, and on it their monarchs laid their hand after the ceremony of coronation, and swore by the sun to safeguard the interests of the empire, and to maintain its customs, traditions and laws. There was a curious prophecy about this block of marble, which was reported among the people to have fallen from the sun, to the effect that when it was shattered into fragments a king of alien race should rule over the land. As the stone, however, looked remarkably solid, the native princes seemed to have a fair chance of keeping their own for many a long year.

At the end of the hall was a daïs spread with rich carpets, on which two thrones were set side by side. These thrones were shaped like great chairs, and made of solid gold. The seats were richly cushioned, but the backs were left bare, and on each was carved the emblem of the sun, shooting out his fiery rays in all directions. The footstools were golden lions couchant, with yellow topazes set in them for eyes. There were no other gems about them.

When we entered we perceived that a large number of

men were gathered together in front of the two thrones, which were unoccupied. The principal among them were seated on carved wooden chairs ranged to the right and the left of the thrones. Seated by themselves, in a little group to the left of the throne were six men of a different stamp. They were clothed in long robes of pure white linen, with the same symbol of the sun that is to be seen on the back of the chairs, emblazoned in gold thread upon the breast.

They were all men of mature age and of a severe and impressive cast of features, which was rendered still more imposing by the long beards they wore.

The personality of one individual among them however impressed us at once. He was very old – eighty at least – and extremely tall, with a long snow-white beard that hung nearly to his waist. His features were aquiline and deeply cut, and his eyes were grey and cold-looking. The heads of the others were bare, but this man wore a round cap entirely covered with gold embroidery, from which we judged that he was a person of great importance; and indeed we after-wards discovered that he was Agon, the High Priest of the country. As we approached, all these men, including the priests, rose and bowed to us with the greatest courtesy, at the same time placing the two fingers across the lips in salutation. Then soft-footed attendants advanced from be-tween the pillars, bearing seats, which were placed in a line in front of the thrones. We three sat down, Alphonse and Umslopogaas standing behind us. Scarcely had we done so when there came a blare of trumpets from some passage to the right, and a similar blare from the left. Next a man with a long white wand of ivory appeared just in front of the right-hand throne, and cried out something in a loud voice, ending with the word *Nyleptha*, repeated three times; and another man, similarly attired, called out a similar sentence before the other throne, but ending with the word *Sorais*, also repeated thrice. Then came the tramp of armed men from each side entrance, and in filed about a score of picked and magnificently accoutred guards, who formed up on each side of the thrones, and let their heavy iron-handled spears fall simultaneously with a clash upon the black marble flooring. Another double blare of trumpets, and in from either side, each attended by six maidens, swept the two Queens of Zu-Vendis, everybody in the hall rising to greet them as they came.

I have seen beautiful women in my day, and am no longer thrown into transports at the sight of a pretty face; but language fails me when I try to give some idea of the blaze of loveliness that then broke upon us in the persons of these sister Queens. Both were young – perhaps five-and-twenty years of age – both were tall and exquisitely formed; but there the likeness stopped. One, Nyleptha, was a woman of dazzling fairness; her right arm and breast bare, after the custom of her people, showed like snow even against her white and gold-embroidered 'kaf', or toga. And as for her sweet face, all I can say is, that it was one that few men could look on and forget. Her hair, a veritable crown of gold, clustered in short ringlets over her shapely head, half hiding the ivory brow, beneath which eyes of deep and glorious grey flashed out in tender majesty. Over the whole countenance there shone an indescribable look of loving kindness.

Her twin sister, Sorais, was of a different and darker type of beauty. Her hair was wavy like Nyleptha's but coal-black and fell in masses on her shoulders; her complexion was olive, her eyes large, dark, and lustrous; the lips were full and I thought rather cruel. Somehow her face, quiet and even cold as it was, gave an idea of passion in repose, and caused one to wonder involuntarily what its aspect would be if anything occurred to break the calm.

As they passed to their seats I saw both of them glance swiftly in our direction. I saw, too, that their eyes passed by me, seeing nothing to charm them in the person of an insignificant and grizzled old man. Then they looked with evident astonishment on the grim form of old Umslopogaas, who raised his axe in salutation. Attracted next by the splendour of Good's apparel, for a second their glance rested on him like a humming moth upon a flower, then off it darted to where Sir Henry Curtis stood, the sunlight from a window playing upon his yellow hair and peaked beard, and marking the outlines of his massive frame against the twilight of the somewhat gloomy hall. He raised his eyes, and they met the fair Nyleptha's full, and thus for the first time the goodliest man and woman that it has ever been my lot to see looked one upon another. And why it was I know not, but I saw the swift blood run up beneath Nyleptha's skin as the pink lights run up the morning sky. I glanced at Sir Henry. He, too, had coloured up to the eyes.

Both the Queens seated themselves on the thrones, the unseen trumpets blared out, and then the Court seated itself, and Queen Sorais motioned to us to do likewise.

Next from among the crowd whither he had withdrawn stepped forward our guide. Having made obeisance he proceeded to address the Queens, evidently describing to them the way and place where we had been found. It was most amusing to watch the astonishment, not unmixed with fear, reflected upon their faces as they listened to his tale. We began to realize that he was talking about the hippopotami we had killed and that there was something very wrong. For the history was frequently interrupted by indignant exclamations from the little group of white-robed priests and even from the courtiers, while the two Queens listened with an amazed expression, especially when our guide pointed to the rifles in our hands as being the means of destruction. And here, to make matters clear, I may as well explain at once that the inhabitants of Zu-Vendis are sun-worshippers, and that for some reason or other the hippopotamus is a sacred animal among them. Now, as ill luck would have it the particular hippopotami we had shot were a family of tame animals that were kept at the mouth of the port and daily fed by priests whose special duty it was to attend to them.

When our guide had finished his tale, the old man with the long beard and round cap rose and commenced an impassioned harangue. I did not like the look of his cold grey eye as he fixed it on us.

After he had finished speaking the Queen Sorais addressed him in a soft and musical voice, and appeared, to judge from his gestures of dissent, to be putting the other side of the question before him. Then Nyleptha spoke in liquid accents. Little did we know that she was pleading for our lives. Finally, she turned and addressed a tall, soldierlike man of middle age with a black beard and a long plain sword, whose name, as we afterwards learnt, was Nasta, and who was the greatest lord in the country; apparently appealing to him for support. Now when Sir Henry had caught her eye and she had blushed so rosy red, I had seen that the incident had not escaped this man's notice, and, what is more, that it was eminently disagreeable to him, for he bit his lip and his hand tightened on his sword-hilt. Afterwards we learnt that he was an aspirant for the hand of this Queen in marriage, which accounted for it. This being so, Nyleptha could not have appealed to a worse person, for, speaking in slow, heavy tones, he appeared to confirm all that the High Priest Agon said.

Nyleptha grew very angry. Her cheek flushed, her eyes flashed, and she did indeed look lovely. Finally she turned to Agon and seemed to give some sort of qualified assent, for he bowed at her words; and as she spoke she moved her hands as though to emphasize what she said; while all the time Sorais kept her chin on her hand and smiled. Then suddenly Nyleptha made a sign, the trumpets blew again, and everybody rose to leave the hall save ourselves and the guards, whom she motioned to stay.

When they were all gone she bent forward and, smiling sweetly, partially by signs and partially by exclamations made it clear to us that she was very anxious to know where we came from. The difficulty was how to explain, but at last an idea struck me. I had my large pocket-book in my pocket and a pencil. Taking it out, I made a little sketch of a lake, and then as best I could drew the underground river and the lake at the other end. When I had done this I advanced to the steps of the throne and gave it to her. She understood it at once and clapped her hands with delight, and then descending from the throne took it to her sister Sorais, who also evidently understood. Next she took the pencil from me, and after examining it with curiosity proceeded to make a series of delightful little sketches, the first representing herself holding out both hands in welcome, and a man uncommonly like Sir Henry taking them. Next she drew a lovely little picture of a hippopotamus rolling about dying in the water, and of an individual, in whom we had no difficulty in recognizing Agon the High Priest holding up his hands in horror on the bank. Then followed a most alarming picture of a dreadful fiery furnace and of the same figure, Agon, poking us into it with a forked stick. This picture perfectly horrified me, but I was a little reassured when she nodded sweetly and proceeded to make a fourth drawing – of a man again uncommonly like Sir Henry, and of two women, in whom I recognized Sorais and herself, each with one arm around him, and holding a sword in protection over him. To all of these Sorais, who I saw was employed in carefully taking us all in – especially Curtis – signified her approval by nodding.

At last Nyleptha drew a final sketch of a rising sun, indicating that she must go, and that we should meet on the following morning; whereat Sir Henry looked so disappointed that she saw it, and, I suppose by way of consolation, extended her hand to him to kiss, which he did with pious fervour. At the same time Sorais, off whom Good had never taken his eyeglass, rewarded him by giving him her hand to kiss, though, while she did so, her eyes were fixed upon Sir Henry. I am glad to say that I was not implicated in these proceedings; neither of them gave *me* her hand to kiss.

When the Queens had gone, an officer came forward and with many tokens of deep respect led us from the hall through various passages to a sumptuous set of apartments opening out of a large central room lighted with brazen swinging lamps and richly carpeted and strewn with couches. On a table in the centre of the room was set a profusion of food and fruit, and, what is more, flowers. There was delicious wine also in ancient-looking sealed earthenware flagons, and beautifully chased golden and ivory cups to drink it from. So very weary were we with our labours that we could scarcely keep ourselves awake through the sumptuous meal, and as soon as it was over we indicated that we desired to sleep. So they led us off, and would have given us a room each, but we made it clear that we would sleep two in a room. As a further precaution against surprise we left Umslopogaas with his axe to sleep in the main chamber near the curtained doorways leading to the apartments which we occupied respectively, Good and I in the one, and Sir Henry and Alphonse in the other. Then throwing off our clothes, with the exception of the mail shirts, which we considered it safer to keep on, we flung ourselves down upon the low and luxurious couches, drew the silk-embroidered coverlids over us, and fell fast asleep.

THIRTEEN
The Flower Temple

It was half-past eight by my watch when I woke on the morning following our arrival at Milosis, having slept almost exactly twelve hours, and I must say that I did indeed feel better.

I sat up upon my silken couch – never had I slept upon such a bed before – and the first thing that I saw was Good's eyeglass fixed on me from the recesses of his silken couch. There was nothing else of him to be seen except his eyeglass, but I knew from the look of it that he was awake, and waiting till I woke. Then, there came a sound at the curtain, which, on being drawn, admitted a functionary, who signified by signs that he was there to lead us to the bath. We gladly consented, and were conducted to a delightful marble chamber, with a pool of running crystal water in the centre of it, into which we gaily plunged. When we had bathed, we returned to our apartment and dressed, and then went into the central room where we had supped on the previous evening, to find a morning meal already prepared for us. After breakfast our friend the captain of the guard presented himself, and with many obeisances signified that we were to follow him, which we did, not without doubts and heart-searchings – for we guessed that the time had come when we should have to settle the bill for those confounded hippopotami with our cold-eyed friend Agon, the High Priest. Indeed we were taken by carriage to the dazzling Temple of the Sun. It is built in the shape of a sunflower, with a dome-covered central hall, from which radiate twelve petal-shaped courts, each dedicated to one of the twelve months, and serving as the repositories of statues reared in memory of the illustrious dead. The building is of pure and polished white marble, which shows out in mar- vellous contrast to the red granite of the frowning city, on whose brow it glistens indeed like an imperial diadem upon the forehead of a dusky queen. The outer surface of the dome and of the twelve petal courts is covered entirely with thin sheets of beaten gold; and from the extreme point of the roof of each of these petals a glorious golden form with a trumpet in its hand and widespread wings is figured in the very act of soaring into space. What makes the whole effect even more gorgeous is that a belt of a hundred and fifty feet around the marble wall of the temple is planted with an indigenous species of sunflower, which were at the time when we first saw them a sheet of golden bloom.

At the temple gates our party was received by a guard of soldiers, who appeared to be under the orders of a priest; and by them we were conducted inside. A priest appeared, and made a sign, and the officer of the guard signified to us that we were expected to advance, which we did with the best grace that we could muster, all except Alphonse, whose irrepressible teeth instantly began to chatter. In a few seconds we were looking at a vast sea of human faces stretching away to the farthest limits of the great circle, all straining to catch a glimpse of the mysterious strangers who had committed sacrilege; the first strangers, mind you, who, to the knowledge of the multitude, had ever set foot in Zu-Vendis since such time that the memory of man runneth not to the contrary.

I looked about me and marvelled at the beauty of the holy place. Above us was a great white marble dome, with a funnel-like opening at the exact apex, from which light poured upon the central golden altar. This altar, in shape round like the sun, four feet in height and thirty-six in circumference, was covered with twelve closed petals of beaten gold.

As we appeared, there was a murmur throughout the vast crowd that went echoing away up the great dome, and we saw a visible blush of excitement grow on the thousands of faces, like a pink light on a stretch of pale cloud, and a very curious effect it was. On we passed down a lane cut through the heart of the human mass, till presently we were led to a patch of flooring, not of pure white marble as elsewhere, but made of solid brass, to the east of the central altar and immediately facing it. For some thirty feet around the space was roped off, and the multitudes stood outside the ropes. Within were a circle of white-robed priests holding long golden trumpets in their hands, and immediately in front of us was our friend Agon, the High Priest. Then came a pause, and I looked around to see if there was any sign of the two Queens, Nyleptha and Sorais, but they were not there. To the right of us, however, was a bare space that I guessed was reserved for them.

We waited, and presently a far-off trumpet blew, apparently high up in the dome. Then came another murmur from the multitude, and up a long lane, leading to the open space to our right, we saw the two Queens walking side by side. Behind them were some nobles of the Court, among whom I recognized the great lord Nasta, and behind them again a body of about fifty guards. These last I was very glad to see. Presently they had all arrived and taken their stand, the two Queens in the front, the nobles to the right and left, and the guards in a double semicircle behind them.

Then came another silence, and Nyleptha looked up and caught my eye; it seemed to me that there was meaning in her glance, and I watched it narrowly. From my eye it travelled down to the brass flooring, on the outer edge of which we stood. Then followed a slight and almost imperceptible sidelong movement of the head. I did not understand it, and it was repeated. Then I guessed that she meant us to move back off the brazen floor. One more glance and I was sure of it – there was danger in standing on the floor. Sir Henry was placed on one side of me, Umslopogaas on the other. Keeping my eyes fixed straight before me, I whispered to them, first in Zulu and then in English, to draw slowly back inch by inch till half their feet were resting on the marble flooring where the brass ceased. Sir Henry whispered on to Good and Alphonse, and slowly, very very slowly, we shifted backwards; so slowly indeed that nobody except Nyleptha and Sorais, who saw everything, seemed to notice the movement. Then I glanced again at Nyleptha, and saw that, by an almost imperceptible nod, she indicated approval. All the while Agon's eyes were fixed upon the altar before him apparently in an ecstasy of contemplation, and mine were fixed upon the small of his back in another sort of ecstasy. Suddenly he flung up his long arms, and in a solemn and resounding voice commenced a chant, which none of us, of course, could understand. When he finished, he glanced up towards the funnel-sloped opening in the dome and added a command I later learnt meant '*Oh Sun, descend upon thine Altar!*'

As he spoke a wonderful and a beautiful thing happened. Down from on high flashed a splendid living ray of light, cleaving the twilight like a sword of fire. Full upon the closed petals of the altar, it fell and ran shimmering down their golden sides, and then the glorious flower opened as though beneath the bright influence. Slowly it opened, and as the great petals fell wide and revealed the golden altar on which the fire ever burns, the priests blew a blast upon the trumpets, and from all the people there rose a shout of praise that beat against the domed roof and came echoing down the marble walls. And now the flower altar was open, and the sunlight fell full upon the tongue of sacred flame and beat it down, so that it wavered, sank, and vanished into the hollow recesses whence it rose. As it vanished, the mellow notes of the trumpets rolled out once more. Again the old priest flung up his hands and called aloud, '*We sacrifice to thee, oh Sun!*'

Once more I caught Nyleptha's eye; it was fixed upon the brazen flooring.

'Look out,' I said, aloud; and as I said it, I saw Agon bend forward and touch something on the altar. As he did so, the great white sea of faces around us turned red and then white again, and a deep breath went up like a universal sigh. Nyleptha leant forward, and with an involuntary movement covered her eyes with her hand. Sorais turned and whispered to the officer of the royal bodyguard, and then with a rending sound the whole of the brazen flooring slid from before our feet, and there in its place was suddenly revealed a smooth marble shaft terminating in a most awful raging furnace beneath the altar.

With a cry of terror we sprang backwards, all except the wretched Alphonse, who was paralysed with fear, and would have fallen into the fiery furnace which had been prepared for us, had not Sir Henry caught him in his strong hand as he was vanishing and dragged him back.

Instantly there arose the most fearful hubbub, and we four got back to back, Alphonse dodging frantically round our little circle in his attempts to take shelter under our legs. We all had our revolvers on – for though we had been politely disarmed of our guns on leaving the palace, of course these people did not know what a revolver was. Umslopogaas, too, had his axe, of which no effort had been made to deprive him, and now he whirled it round his head and sent his piercing Zulu war-shout echoing up the marble walls in fine defiant fashion. Next second, the priests, baffled of their prey, had drawn swords from beneath their white robes and were leaping on us like hounds upon a stag at bay. I saw that, dangerous as action might be, we must act or be lost, so as the first man came bounding along – and a great tall fellow he was – I sent a heavy revolver ball through him, and down he fell at the mouth of the shaft, an slid, shrieking frantically, into the fiery gulf that had been prepared for us.

Whether it was his cries, or the, to them, awful sound and effect of the pistol shot, or what, I know not, but the other priests halted, paralysed and dismayed, and before they could come on again Sorais had called out something, and we, together with the two Queens and most of the courtiers, were being surrounded with a wall of armed men.

The last yell of the burning priest died away, the fire had finished him, and a great silence fell upon the place.

Then the High Priest Agon turned, and his face was as the face of a devil. Afterwards we learnt the meaning of all that followed. 'Let the sacrifice be sacrificed,' he cried to the Queens. 'Has not sacrilege enough been done by these strangers, and would ye, as Queens, throw the cloak of your majesty over evildoers? Are not the creatures sacred to the Sun dead and is not a priest of the Sun also dead, but now slain by the magic of these strangers, who come as the winds out of heaven, whence we know not, and who are what we know not? Let the sacrifice be sacrificed, oh Queens.'

Then Sorais made answer in her deep quiet tones, that always seemed to me to have a suspicion of mockery about them, however serious the theme: 'Oh, Agon the midday sacrifice is accomplished; the Sun hath claimed his priest as a sacrifice.'

This was a novel idea, and the people applauded it.

'What are these men? They are strangers found floating on the bosom of a lake. Who brought them there? How came they there? How know you that they also are not servants of the Sun? Is this the hospitality that ye would have our nation show to those whom chance brings to them, to throw them to the flames? Shame on you!' She paused a little to watch the effect of her speech upon the multitude, and seeing that it was favourable, changed her tone from one of remonstrance to one of command.

'Ho! place there,' she cried; 'place, I say; make way for the Queens, and those whom the Queens cover with their "kaf" (mantle).'

'And if I refuse, oh Queen?' said Agon between his teeth.

'Then will I cut a path with my guards,' was the proud answer; 'ay, even in the presence of the sanctuary, and through the bodies of thy priests.'

Agon turned livid with baffled fury. He glanced at the people as though meditating an appeal to them, but saw clearly that their sympathies were all the other way.

Then for the first time Nyleptha spoke in her soft sweet voice.

'Bethink thee, Agon,' she said, 'as my sister Queen hath said, these men may also be servants of the Sun. For themselves they cannot speak, for their tongues are tied. Let the matter be adjourned till such time as they have learnt our language.'

Here was a clever loophole of escape, and the vindictive old priest took it, little as he liked it.

'So be it, oh Queens,' he said. 'Let the men go in peace, and when they have learnt our tongue then let them speak.'

These words were received with a murmur of applause,

and in another minute we were marching out of the temple surrounded by the royal guards.

But it was not till long afterwards that we learnt the exact substance of what had passed, and how hardly our lives had been wrung out of the cruel grip of the Zu-Vendi priesthood, in the face of which even the Queens were practically powerless. Had it not been for their strenuous efforts to protect us we should have been slain even before we set foot in the Temple of the Sun. The attempt to drop us bodily into the fiery pit as an offering was a last artifice to attain this end when several others quite unsuspected by us had already failed.

FOURTEEN
The Proposal

After our escape from Agon and his pious crew we returned to our quarters in the palace and had a very good time. The two Queens, the nobles and the people vied with each other in doing us honour and showering gifts upon us. Every day deputations and individuals waited on us to examine our guns and clothing, our chain shirts, and our instruments, especially our watches, with which they were much delighted. In short, we became quite the rage, so much so that some of the fashionable young swells among the Zu-Vendi began to copy the cut of some of our clothes, notably Sir Henry's shooting jacket.

Meanwhile we pursued our study of the language steadily and made very good progress. On the morning following our adventure in the temple three grave and reverend signiors presented themselves armed with manuscript books, ink-horns, and feather pens, and indicated that they had been sent to teach us. So, with the exception of Umslopogaas, we all buckled to with a will, doing four hours a day. As for Umslopogaas, he would have none of that either. He did not wish to learn that 'woman's talk', not he; and when one of the teachers advanced on him with a book, he sprang up with a fierce oath and flashed Inkosi-kaas before the eyes of our learned friend, and there was an end of the attempt to teach *him* Zu-Vendi.

Some days we would pay visits to the country seats at some of the great lords' beautiful fortified places, and the villages clustering beneath their walls. Here we saw vine yards and cornfields and well-kept park-like grounds, with such timber in them as filled me with delight, for I do love a good tree.

In the evenings it was customary for Sir Henry, Good, and myself to dine, or rather sup, with their Majesties—not every night, indeed, but about three or four times a week, whenever they had not much company, or the affairs of state would allow it. Over the weeks it became clear to me that Nyleptha was falling in love with that brave, good friend of mine, Sir Henry Curtis. More than that: I knew, though he never spoke of it, that he was falling in love with the fair Queen.

Evenings spent with their Majesties were jolly affairs. All the while that we talked and laughed, Sorais would sit there in her carven ivory chair, and look at us and read us all like a book, only from time to time saying a few words, and smiling that quick ominous smile of hers which was more like a flash of summer lightning on a dark cloud than anything else. And as near to her as he dared would sit Good, worshipping through his eyeglass, for he really was getting seriously devoted to this sombre beauty, of whom, speaking personally, I felt terribly afraid. I watched her keenly, and soon I found out that for all her apparent impassibility she was at heart bitterly jealous of Nyleptha. Another thing I found out, and the discovery filled me with dismay, and that was, that she *also* was growing devoted to Sir Henry Curtis.

And so another three months passed over us, by which time we had all attained to a very considerable mastery of the Zu-Vendi language, which is an easy one to learn. And as the time went on we became great favourites with the people. We were advanced to great honour and made officers of the bodyguards of the sister Queens, while permanent quarters were assigned to us in the palace, and our opinion was asked upon questions of national policy.

But blue as the sky seemed, there was a cloud, and a big one, on the horizon. We had indeed heard no more of those confounded hippopotami, but it is not on that account to be supposed that our sacrilege was forgotten, or the enmity of the great and powerful priesthood headed by Agon appeased. On the contrary, it was burning the more fiercely because it was necessarily suppressed, and what had perhaps begun in bigotry was ending in downright direct hatred born of jealousy. Hitherto, the priests had been the wise men of the land, and were on this account, as well as from superstitious causes, looked on with peculiar veneration. But our arrival, with our outlandish wisdom and our strange inventions and hints of unimagined things, dealt a serious blow to this state of affairs, and, among the educated Zu-Vendi, went far towards destroying the priestly prestige.

Another source of imminent danger to us was the rising envy of some of the great lords headed by Nasta, whose antagonism to us had at best been but thinly veiled, and which now threatened to break out into open flame. Nasta had for some years been a candidate for Nyleptha's hand in marriage, and when we appeared on the scene I fancy, from all I could gather, that though there will still many obstacles in his path, success was by no means out of his reach. But now all this had changed; the coy Nyleptha smiled no more in his direction, and he was not slow to guess the cause.

So Nasta bethought him of the thirty thousand wild

swordsmen who would pour down at his bidding through the northern mountain passes, and no doubt vowed to adorn the gates of Milosis with our heads.

But first he determined, as we learned, to make one more attempt and to demand the hand of Nyleptha in the open Court after the formal annual ceremony of the signing of the laws that had been proclaimed by the Queens during the year.

Of this astounding fact Nyleptha heard with simulated nonchalance, and with a little trembling of the voice herself informed us of it as we sat at supper on the night preceding the great ceremony of the law-signing.

Sir Henry bit his lip, and do what he could to prevent it plainly showed his agitation.

'And what answer will the Queen be pleased to give to the great Lord?' asked I, in a jesting manner.

'Answer, Macumazahn' (for we had elected to pass by our Zulu names in Zu-Vendis), she said, with a pretty shrug of her ivory shoulder. 'Nay, I know not; what is a poor woman to do, when the wooer has thirty thousand swords wherewith to urge his love?' And from under her long lashes she glanced at Curtis.

Just then we rose from the table to adjourn into another room. 'Quatermain, a word, quick,' said Sir Henry to me. 'Listen. I have never spoken about it, but surely you have guessed: I love Nyleptha. What am I to do?'

'You must speak to Nyleptha to-night,' I said. 'Now is your time, now or never. Listen. In the sitting-chamber get near to her, and whisper to her to meet you at midnight by the Rademas statue at the end of the great hall. I will keep watch for you there. Now or never, Curtis.'

The time went on; in another quarter of an hour I knew that, according to their habit, the Queens would retire. As yet, Sir Henry had had no chance of saying a word in private: indeed, though we saw much of the royal sisters, it was by no means easy to see them alone. I racked my brains, and at last an idea came to me.

'Will the Queen be pleased,' I said, bowing low before Sorais, 'to sing unto her servants? Our hearts are heavy this night; sing to us, oh Lady of the Night' (Sorais' favourite name among the people).

'My songs, Macumazahn, are not such as to lighten the heavy heart, yet will I sing if it pleases thee,' she answered; and she rose and went a few paces to a table whereon lay an instrument not unlike a zither, and struck a few wandering chords.

Then suddenly, like the notes of some deep-throated bird, her rounded voice rang out in song so wildly sweet, and yet with so eerie and sad a refrain, that it made the very blood stand still.

'Now, Curtis, now,' I whispered, when she began to sing, and turned my back.

'Nyleptha,' he said – for my nerves were so much on the stretch that I could hear every word, low as it was spoken, even through Sorais' divine notes – 'Nyleptha, I must speak with thee this night, upon my life I must.'

'How can I speak with thee?' she answered, looking fixedly before her; 'Queens are not like other people. I am surrounded and watched.'

'Listen, Nyleptha, thus. I will be before the statue of Rademas in the great hall at midnight.'

'It is not seemly,' she murmured, 'and tomorrow—'

Just then the music began to die in the last wail of the refrain, and Sorais slowly turned her head round.

'I will be there,' said Nyleptha, hurriedly; 'on thy life see that thou fail me not.'

FIFTEEN

Before The Statue

It was night – dead night – and the silence lay on the Frowning City like a cloud.

Secretly, as evildoers, Sir Henry Curtis, Umslopogaas, and myself threaded our way through the passages towards a by-entrance to the great Throne Chamber. Once we were met by the fierce rattling challenge of the sentry. I gave the countersign, and the man grounded his spear and let us pass. Also we were officers of the Queen's bodyguard, and in that capacity had a right to come and go unquestioned.

We gained the hall in safety. So empty and so still was it, that even when we had passed the sound of our footsteps yet echoed up the lofty walls, vibrating faintly and still more faintly against the carven roof, like ghosts of the footsteps of dead men haunting the place that once they trod.

By the statue of Rademas we took our stand, and waited. Sir Henry and I close together, Umslopogaas some paces off in the darkness, so that I could only just make out his towering outline leaning on the outline of an axe. Then from far far away there came a little sound as though the statues that lined the walls were whispering to each other some message of the ages.

It was the faint sweep of a lady's dress. Nearer it grew, and nearer yet. We could see a figure steal from patch to patch of moonlight, and even hear the soft fall of sandalled feet. Another second and I saw the black silhouette of the old Zulu raise its arm in mute salute, and Nyleptha was before us.

Oh, how beautiful she looked as she paused a moment just within the circle of the moonlight! Low we bowed before her, and then she spoke.

'I have come,' she whispered, 'but it was at great risk. Ye know not how I am watched. Thou didst bid me come hither, my Lord Incubu' (Curtis had taught her to call him so). 'Doubtless it is about business of the State, for I know that thou art ever full of great ideas and plans for my welfare and my people's. So even as a Queen should I have come, though I greatly fear the dark alone,' and again she laughed and gave him a glance from her grey eyes.

At this point I thought it wise to move a little, since secrets 'of the State' should not be made public property; but she would not let me go far, peremptorily stopping me within five yards or so, saying that she feared surprise. So it came to pass that, however unwillingly, I heard all that passed.

'Thou knowest, Nyleptha,' said Sir Henry, 'that it was for none of these things that I asked thee to meet me at this lonely place. Nyleptha, waste not the time in pleasantry, but listen to me, for – I love thee.'

As he said the words I saw her face break up, as it were, and change. The coquetry went out of it, and in its place there shone a great light of love which seemed to glorify it.

'Thou sayest thou dost love me,' she said in a low voice, 'and thy voice rings true, but how am I to know that thou dost speak the truth?

'Though,' she went on with proud humility, and in the stately third person which is so largely used by the Zu-Vendi, 'I be as nothing in the eyes of my lord,' and she curtseyed towards him, 'who comes from among a wonderful people, to whom my people are but children, yet here am I a queen and a leader of men. And although my beauty be a little thing in the eyes of my lord,' and she lifted her broidered skirt and curtseyed again, 'yet here among my own people am I held right fair, and ever since I was a woman the great lords of my kingdom have made quarrel concerning me. Let my lord pardon me if I weary my lord, but it hath pleased my lord to say that he loves me, Nyleptha, a Queen of the Zu-Vendi, and therefore would I say that though my love and my hand be not much to my lord, yet to me are they all.'

'Nyleptha,' answered Sir Henry, adopting the Zu-Vendi way of speech; 'I have told thee that I love thee; how am I to tell thee how much I love thee? Is there then a measure for love? Yet will I try. I say not that I have never looked upon another woman with favour, but this I say that I love thee with all my life and with all my strength; that I love thee now and shall love thee till I grow cold in death, ay, and as I believe beyond my death, and on and on for ever. Now for thy dear sake I will forget my people and my father's house, yea, I renounce them all. By thy side will I live, Nyleptha, and at thy side will I die.'

Slowly, slowly she raised her head, and fixed her wonderful eyes, all alight with the greatness of her passion, full upon his face, as though to read his very soul. Then at last she spoke, low indeed, but clearly as a silver bell.

'Of a truth, weak woman that I am, I do believe thee. And now hearken unto me, oh man, who hath wandered here from far to steal my heart and make me all thine own. I put my hand upon thy hand thus, and thus I, whose lips have never kissed before, do kiss thee on the brow; and now by my hand and by that first and holy kiss, ay, by my people's weal and by my throne that like enough I shall lose for thee – by the name of my high House, by the sacred Stone and by the eternal majesty of the Sun, I swear that for thee will I live and die. Even at thy feet I do my homage;' and the lovely impassioned creature flung herself down on her knees on the cold marble before him. I could stand it no longer, and cleared off to refresh myself with a little of old Umslopogaas' society, leaving them to settle it their own way, and a very long time they were about it.

Some three-quarters of an hour afterwards the 'pair of doves' came strolling towards us, Curtis looking slightly silly, and Nyleptha remarking calmly that the moonlight made very pretty effects on the marble. Then, for she was in a most gracious mood, she took my hand and said that I was 'her Lord's' dear friend, and therefore dear to her. Next she lifted Umslopogaas' axe, and examined it curiously, saying significantly as she did so that he might soon have cause to use it in defence of her.

After that she nodded prettily to us all, and casting one tender glance at her lover, glided off into the darkness like a beautiful vision.

On the following morning Good was informed of the happy occurrence, and positively rippled with smiles. The fact of the matter was that not only was Good rejoiced about the thing on its own merits but also for personal reasons. He adored Sorais quite as earnestly as Sir Henry adored Nyleptha, and his adoration had not altogether prospered. Indeed, it had seemed to him and to me also that the dark Cleopatra-like queen favoured Curtis in her own curious inscrutable way much more than Good. Therefore it was a relief to him to learn that his unconscious rival was permanently and satisfactorily attached in another direction. His face fell a little, however, when he was told that the whole thing was to be kept as secret as the dead, above all from Sorais for the present.

That morning we again attended in the Throne Hall, and I could not help smiling to myself when I compared the visit to our last, and reflecting that, if walls could speak, they would have strange tales to tell.

What actresses women are! There, high upon her golden throne, draped in her blazoned 'kaf' or robe of state, sat the fair Nyleptha, and when Sir Henry came in a little late, dressed in the full uniform of an officer of her guard and humbly bent himself before her, she merely acknowledged his salute with a careless nod and turned her head coldly aside. It was a very large Court, for not only did the ceremony of signing of the laws attract many outside of those whose duty it was to attend, but also the rumour that Nasta was going to publicly ask the hand of Nyleptha in marriage had gone abroad, with the result that the great hall was crowded to its utmost capacity.

Nasta stepped forward and bowing humbly, though with no humility in his eye, craved a boon at the hands of the Queen Nyleptha.

Nyleptha turned a little pale, but bowed graciously, and prayed the 'well-beloved lord' to speak on, whereon in a few straightforward soldier-like words he asked her hand in marriage.

Then, before she could find words to answer, the high priest Agon took up the tale, and in a speech of real eloquence and power pointed out the many advantages of the proposed alliance.

When he had finished, Nyleptha prepared herself to answer. Before she did so, however, Sorais leant towards her and said in a voice sufficiently loud for me to catch what she said, 'Bethink thee well, my sister, ere thou dost speak, for methinks that our thrones may hang upon thy words.'

Nyleptha made no answer, and with a shrug and a smile Sorais leant back again and listened.

'Of a truth a great honour has been done to me,' she said, 'that my poor hand should not only have been asked in marriage, but that Agon here should be so swift to pronounce the blessing of the Sun upon my union. Nasta, I thank thee, and I will bethink me of thy words, but now as yet I have no mind for marriage, that is a cup of which none know the taste until they begin to drink it. Again I thank thee, Nasta,' and she made as though she would rise.

The great lord's face turned almost as black as his beard with fury, for he knew that the words amounted to a final refusal of his suit.

'Thanks be to the Queen for her gracious words,' he said, restraining himself with difficulty and looking anything but grateful, 'my heart shall surely treasure them. And now I crave another boon, namely, the royal leave to withdraw myself to my own poor cities in the north till such time as the Queen shall say my suit nay or yea. Mayhap,' he added, with a sneer, 'the Queen will be pleased to visit me there, and to bring with her these stranger lords,' and he scowled darkly towards us. 'It is but a poor country and a rough, but we are a hardy race of mountaineers, and there shall be gathered thirty thousand swordsmen to shout a welcome to her.'

This speech, which was almost a declaration of rebellion, was received in complete silence, but Nyleptha flushed up and answered it with spirit.

'Oh, surely, Nasta, I will come, and the strange lords in my train, and for every man of thy mountaineers who calls thee Prince, will I bring two from the lowlands who call me Queen, and we will see which is the staunchest breed. Till then farewell.'

The trumpets blared out, the Queens rose, and the great assembly broke up in murmuring confusion, and for myself I went home with a heavy heart foreseeing civil war.

After this there was quiet for a few weeks. Curtis and the Queen did not often meet, and exercised the utmost caution not to allow the true relation in which they stood to each other to leak out; but do what they would, rumours as hard to trace as a buzzing fly in a dark room, and yet quite as audible, began to hum round and round, and at last to settle on her throne.

SIXTEEN

The Storm Breaks

And now it was that the trouble which at first had been but a cloud as large as a man's hand began to loom very black and big upon our horizon, namely, Sorais' preference for Sir Henry. I saw the storm drawing nearer and nearer; and so, poor fellow, did he. The affection of so lovely and highly-placed a woman was not a thing that could in a general way be considered a calamity by any man, but, situated as Curtis was, it was a grievous burden to bear.

The more Sir Henry held off the more Sorais came on, as is not uncommon in such cases, till at last things got very queer indeed. Evidently she was, by some strange perversity of mind, quite blinded to the true state of the case; and I, for one, greatly dreaded the moment of her awakening. Sorais was a dangerous woman to be mixed up with, either with or without one's own consent. At last the evil moment came, as I saw it must come. One fine day, Good having gone out hawking, Sir Henry and I were sitting quietly talking over the situation, especially with reference to Sorais, when a Court messenger arrived with a written note, which we with some difficulty deciphered, and which was to the effect that 'the Queen Sorais commanded the attendance of the Lord Incubu in her private apartments, whither he would be conducted by the bearer.'

'What right has this Queen to command my attendance, I should like to know? I won't go,' said Sir Henry.

'But you must,' I said, 'you are one of her officers and bound to obey her, and she knows it.'

'I only hope she won't put a knife into me. I believe that she is quite capable of it.' And off he started very faint-heartedly, and no wonder.

I sat and waited, and at the end of about forty-five minutes he returned, looking a great deal worse than when he went.

'Give me something to drink,' he said hoarsely.

I got him a cup of wine, and asked what was the matter.

'What is the matter? Why if ever there was trouble there's trouble now. You know when I left you? Well, I was shown straight into Sorais' private chamber, and a wonderful place it is; and there she sat, quite alone, upon a silken couch at the end of the room, playing gently upon that zither of hers. I stood before her, and for a while she took no notice of me, but kept on playing and singing a little, and very sweet music it was. At last she looked up and smiled.

'"So thou art come," she said. "I thought that perchance thou hadst gone about the Queen Nyleptha's business. Thou art ever on her business, and I doubt not a good servant and a true."

'To this I merely bowed, and said I was there to receive the Queen's word.

'"Ah yes, I would talk with thee, but be thou seated. It wearies me to look so high," and she made room for me beside her on the couch, placing herself with her back against the end, so as to have a view of my face.

'"It is not meet," I said, "that I should make myself equal with the Queen."

'"I said be seated," was her answer, so I sat down, and she began to look at me with those dark eyes of hers. There she sat like an incarnate spirit of beauty, hardly talking at all, and when she did, very low, but all the while looking at me. There was a white flower in her black hair, and I tried to keep my eyes on it and count the petals, but it was of no use. At last, whether it was her gaze, or the perfume on her hair, or what I do not know, but I almost felt as though I was being mesmerized. At last she roused herself.

'"Incubu," she said, "lovest thou power?"

'I replied that I supposed all men loved power of one sort or another.

'"Thou shalt have it," she said. "Lovest thou wealth?"

'I said I liked wealth for what it brought.

'"Thou shalt have it," she said. "And lovest thou beauty?"

'To this I replied that I was very fond of statuary and architecture, or something silly of that sort, at which she frowned, and there was a pause. By this time my nerves were on such a stretch that I was shaking like a leaf. I knew that something awful was going to happen, but she held me under a kind of spell, and I could not help myself.

'"Incubu," she said at length, "wouldst thou be a king? Listen, wouldst thou be a king? Behold, stranger, I am minded to make thee king of all Zu-Vendis, ay and husband of Sorais of the Night. Nay, peace and hear me. To no man among my people had I thus opened out my secret heart, but thou art an outlander and therefore do I speak without shame, knowing all I have to offer and how hard it had been to thee to ask. See, a crown lies at thy feet, my lord Incubu, and with that fortune a woman whom some have wished to woo. Now mayst thou answer, oh my chosen, and soft shall thy words fall upon mine ears."

'"Oh Sorais," I said, "I pray thee speak not thus" – you see I had not time to pick and choose my words – "for this thing cannot be. I am betrothed to thy sister Nyleptha, oh Sorais, and I love her and her alone."

'Next moment it struck me that I had said an awful thing, and I looked up to see the results. When I spoke, Sorais' face was hidden in her hands, and as my words reached her she slowly raised it, and I shrank back dismayed. It was ashy white, and her eyes were flaming. She rose to her feet and seemed to be choking, but the awful thing was that she was so quiet about it all. Once she looked at a side table, on which lay a dagger, and from it to me, as though she thought of killing me; but she did not take it up. At last she spoke one word, and one only –

'"*Go!*"

'And I went, and glad enough I was to get out of it, and here I am. Give me another cup of wine, there's a good fellow, and tell me, what is to be done?'

I shook my head, for the affair was indeed serious. As one of the poets says,

> 'Hell hath no fury like a woman scorned,'

more especially if the woman is a queen and a Sorais, and indeed I feared the very worst, including imminent danger to ourselves.

'Nyleptha must be told of all this at once,' I said, 'and perhaps I had better tell her; she might receive your account with suspicion.'

'Who is captain of her guard to-night?' I went on.

'Good.'

'Very well then, there will be no chance of her being got at. Don't look surprised. I don't think that her sister would stick at that. I suppose one must tell Good of what has happened.'

'Oh, I don't know,' said Sir Henry. 'It would hurt his

feelings, poor fellow! You see, he takes a lively personal interest in Sorais.'

'That's true; and after all, perhaps there is no need to tell him. He will find out the truth soon enough. Now, you mark my words, Sorais will throw in her lot with Nasta, who is sulking up in the North there, and there will be such a war as has not been known in Zu-Vendis for centuries. Look there!' and I pointed to two Court messengers, who were speeding away from the door of Sorais' private apartments. 'Now follow me,' and I ran up a stairway into an outlook tower that rose from the roof of our quarters, taking the spy-glass with me, and looked out over the palace wall. The first thing we saw was one of the messengers speeding towards the Temple, bearing, without any doubt, the Queen's word to the high priest Agon, but for the other I searched in vain. Presently, however, I spied a horseman riding furiously through the northern gate of the city, and in him I recognized the other messenger.

'Ah!' I said, 'Sorais is a woman of spirit. She is acting at once, and will strike quick and hard. You have insulted her, my boy, and the blood will flow in rivers before the stain is washed away, and yours with it, if she can get hold of you. Well, I'm off to Nyleptha. Just you stop where you are, old fellow, and try to get your nerves straight again.'

I gained audience of the Queen without trouble.

'Is there aught wrong with my Lord, Macumazahn, that he waits not upon me? Say, is he sick?'

I said that he was well enough, and then, without further ado, I plunged into my story and told it from beginning to end.

'And thou thinkest that my sister Sorais would levy war upon me?' she said. 'So be it. She shall not prevail against me. I, too, have my friends and my retainers. There are many, I say, who will shout "Nyleptha!" when my pennon runs up on peak and pinnacle, and the light of my beacon fires leaps to-night from crag to crag, bearing the message of my war. Give me that parchment and the ink. So. Now summon me the officer in the ante-room.'

I did as I was bid! and the man, a veteran and quiet-looking gentleman of the guard, named Kara, entered, bowing low.

'Take this parchment,' said Nyleptha; 'it is thy warrant; and guard every place of in and outgoing in the apartments of my sister Sorais, the "Lady of the Night," and a Queen of the Zu-Vendi. Let none come in and none go out, or thy life shall pay the cost.'

The man looked startled, but he merely said, 'The Queen's word be done,' and departed. Then Nyleptha sent a messenger to Sir Henry.

Curtis arrived and the officer returned, reporting that Sorais was *gone*. The bird had flown to the temple, stating that she was going, as was sometimes the custom among Zu-Vendi ladies of rank, to spend the night in meditation before the altar. We looked at each other significantly. The blow had fallen very soon.

Then we set to work.

Generals who could be trusted were summoned from their quarters, and as much of the State affairs as was thought desirable was told to each, strict injunctions being given to them to get all their available force together. The same was done with such of the more powerful lords as Nyleptha knew she could rely on, several of whom left that very day for distant parts of the country to gather up their tribesmen and retainers. Sealed orders were dispatched to the rulers of far-off-cities.

All the afternoon and evening we laboured, assisted by some confidential scribes, Nyleptha showing an energy and resource of mind that astonished me, and it was eight o'clock before we got back to our quarters. Here we heard from Alphonse that Good had come back from his hawking and gone on duty. As instructions had already been given to the officer of the outer guard to double the sentries at the gate, and as we had no reason to fear any immediate danger, we did not think it worth while to hunt him up and tell him anything of what had passed. After swallowing our food we turned in to get some much-needed rest. Before we did so, however, it ocurred to Curtis to tell old Umslopogaas to keep a look-out in the neighbourhood of Nyleptha's private apartments. Without any comment the Zulu took up his axe and departed, and we also departed to bed.

I seemed to have been asleep but a few minutes when I was awakened by a peculiar sensation of uneasiness. I felt that somebody was in the room and looking at me, and instantly sat up, to see to my surprise that it was already dawn, and that there, standing at the foot of my couch and looking peculiarly grim and gaunt in the grey light, was Umslopogaas himself.

'How long hast thou been there?' I asked testily, for it is not pleasant to be aroused in such a fashion.

'Mayhap the half of an hour, Macumazahn. I have a word for thee.'

'Speak on,' I said, now wide enough awake.

'As I was bid I went last night to the place of the White Queen and hid myself behind a pillar in the second ante-room, beyond which is the sleeping-place of the Queen. There I waited for many hours, when suddenly I perceived a dark figure coming secretly towards me. It was the figure of a woman, and in her hand she held a dagger. Behind that figure crept another unseen by the woman. It was Bougwan following in her tracks.'

'Who was the woman?' I asked impatiently.

'The face was the face of the "Lady of the Night", and of a truth she is well named.

'I waited, and Bougwan passed me also. Then I followed. So we went slowly and without a sound up the long chamber. First the woman, then Bougwan, and then I; and the woman saw not Bougwan, and Bougwan saw not me. At last the "Lady of the Night" came to the curtains that shut off the sleeping place of the White Queen, and put out her left hand to part them. She passed through, and so did Bougwan, and so did I. At the far end of the room is the bed of the Queen, and on it she lay very fast asleep. The "Lady of the Night" doubled herself thus, and with the long knife lifted crept towards the bed. When she was quite close Bougwan touched her on the arm, and she caught her breath and turned, and I saw the knife flash, and heard it strike. Well was it for Bougwan that he had the skin of iron on him, or he had been pierced. Then for the first time he saw who the woman was, and without a word he fell back astonished, and unable to speak. She, too, was astonished, and spoke not, but suddenly she laid her finger on her lip, thus, and walked towards and through the curtain, and with her went Bougwan. So close did she pass to me that her dress touched me, and I was nigh to slaying her as she went. In the first outer room she spoke to Bougwan in a whisper and, clasping her hands thus, she pleaded with him, but what she said I know not. And so they passed on to the second outer room, she pleading and he shaking his head, and saying, "Nay, nay, nay." And it seemed to me that he was about to call the guard, when she stopped talking and looked at him with great eyes, and I saw that he was bewitched by her beauty. Then she stretched out her hand and he kissed it, whereon I gathered myself together to advance and take her, seeing that now had Bougwan become a woman, and no longer knew the good from the evil, when behold! she was gone.'

'Gone!' I ejaculated.

'Ay, gone, and there stood Bougwan staring at the wall like one asleep, and presently he went too, and I waited a while and came away also.'

'Art thou sure, Umslopogaas,' said I, 'that thou hast not been a dreamer this night?'

In reply he opened his left hand, and produced about three inches of the blade of a dagger of the finest steel. 'If I be, Macumazahn, behold what the dream left with me. The knife broke upon Bougwan's bosom, and as I passed I picked this up in the sleeping-place of the White Queen.'

SEVENTEEN
War! Red War!

Telling Umslopogaas to wait, I tumbled into my clothes and went off with him to Sir Henry's room, where the Zulu repeated his story word for word. It was a sight to watch Curtis's face as he heard it.

'Great Heavens!' he said: 'here have I been sleeping away while Nyleptha was nearly murdered – and all through me, too. What a fiend that Sorais must be! It would have served her well if Umslopogaas had cut her down in the act.'

'Ay,' said the Zulu. 'Fear not; I should have slain her ere she struck. I was but waiting the moment.'

I said nothing; but I could not help thinking that many a thousand doomed lives would have been saved if he had meted out to Sorais the fate she meant for her sister. And, as the issue proved, I was right.

Just then Good arrived looking very pale and hollow-eyed.

The moment Umslopogaas saw Good, he greeted him with great enthusiasm.

'Ah, Bougwan,' he cried, 'greeting to thee, Inkoos! Thou art surely weary. Didst thou hunt too much yesterday?' Then, without waiting for an answer, he went on –

'Listen, Bougwan, and I will tell thee a story; it is about a woman, therefore wilt thou hear it, is it not so?

'There was a man and he had a brother, and there was a woman who loved the man's brother and was beloved of the man. But the man's brother had a favourite wife and loved not the woman, and he made a mock of her. Then the woman, being very cunning and fierce-hearted for revenge, took counsel with herself and said to the man, "I love thee, and if thou wilt make war upon thy brother I will marry thee." And he knew it was a lie, yet because of his great love of the woman, who was very fair, did he listen to her words and made war. And when many people had been killed his brother sent to him, saying, "Why slayest thou me? What hurt have I done unto thee, my brother, son of my own mother?"

'Then the man's heart was heavy, and he knew that his path was evil, and he put aside the tempting of the woman and ceased to make war on his brother, and lived at peace in the same kraal with him. And after a time the woman came to him and said, "I have lost the past, I will be thy wife." And in his heart he knew that it was a lie and that she thought the evil thing yet because of his love did he take her to wife.

'And the very night that they were wed, when the man was plunged into a deep sleep, did the woman arise and take his axe from his hand and creep into the hut of his brother and slay him in his rest. Then did she slink back like a gorged lioness and place the thong of the red axe back upon his wrist and go her ways.

'And at the dawning the people came shouting, "Lousta is slain in the night," and they came unto the hut of the man, and there he lay asleep and by him was the red axe.

They would have taken and killed him, but he rose and fled swiftly, and as he fleeted by he slew the woman.

'But death could not wipe out the evil she had done, and on him rested the weight of all her sin. Therefore is he an outcast and his name a scorn among his own people. His name is accursed from generation to generation, in that the people say that he slew his brother, Lousta, by treachery in the night-time.'

The old Zulu paused, and I saw that he was deeply agitated by his own story. Presently he lifted his head, which he had bowed to his breast, and went on:

'I was that man, Bougwan. *I* was that man, and now hark thou! Even as I am so wilt thou be. When thou didst creep after the "Lady of the Night" *I* was hard upon thy track. When she struck thee with the knife in the sleeping place of the White Queen *I* was there also; when thou didst let her slip away like a snake in the stones *I* saw thee, and I knew that she had bewitched thee and that a true man had abandoned the truth. Forgive me, my father, if my words are sharp, but out of a full heart are they spoken. See her no more, so shalt thou go down with honour to the grave. Else because of the beauty of a woman that weareth as a garment of fur shalt thou be even as I am, and perchance with more cause. I have said.'

Throughout this long and eloquent address Good had been perfectly silent, but when the tale began to shape itself so aptly to his own case, he coloured up, and when he learnt that what had passed between him and Sorais had been overseen he was evidently much distressed.

'I must say,' he said, with a bitter little laugh, 'that I scarcely thought that I should live to be taught my duty by a Zulu. I wonder if you fellows can understand how humiliated I feel, and the bitterest part of it is that I deserve it all. Of course I should have handed Sorais over to the guard, but I could not, and that is a fact. I let her go and I promised to say nothing, more is the shame to me. She told me that if I would side with her she would marry me and make me king of this country, but thank goodness I did find the heart to say that even to marry her I could not desert my friends. And now you can do what you like, I deserve it all. All I have to say is that I hope that you may never love a woman with all your heart and then be so sorely tempted of her,' and he turned to go.

'Look here, old fellow,' said Sir Henry, 'just stop a minute. I have a little tale to tell you.' And he went on to narrate what had taken place on the previous day between Sorais and himself.

This was a finishing stroke to poor Good. It is not pleasant to any man to learn that he has been made a fool of.

'Do you know,' he said, 'I think that between you, you fellows have about worked a cure,' and he turned and walked away, and I for one felt very sorry for him.

That day was a Court day, when the Queens sat in the great hall and received petitions, discussed laws, money grants, and so forth, and thither we adjourned shortly afterwards. When we got into the hall Nyleptha was already on her throne and proceeding with business as usual, surrounded by councillors, courtiers, lawyers, priests, and an unusually strong guard. It was, however, easy to see from the air of excitement and expectation on the faces of everybody present that nobody was paying much attention to ordinary affairs.

We saluted Nyleptha and took our accustomed places, and for a little while things went on as usual, when suddenly the trumpets began to call outside the palace, and from the great crowd that was gathered there in anticipation of some unusual event there rose a roar of '*Sorais! Sorais!*'

Then came the roll of many chariot wheels, and presently the great curtains at the end of the hall were drawn wide and through them entered the 'Lady of the Night' herself. Nor did she come alone. Preceding her was Agon, and on either side were other priests. The reason for their presence was obvious – coming with them it would have been sacrilege to attempt to detain her. Behind her were a number of the great lords, and behind them a small body of picked guards. A glance at Sorais herself was enough to show that her mission was of no peaceful kind, for in place of her gold-embroidered 'kaf' she wore a shining tunic formed of golden scales, and on her head a little golden helmet. In her hand, too, she bore a toy spear, beautifully made and fashioned of solid silver. Up the hall she came looking like a lioness in her conscious pride and beauty, and as she came the spectators fell back bowing and made a path for her. By the sacred stone she halted, and laying her hand on it, she cried out with a loud voice to Nyleptha on the throne, 'Hail, oh Queen!'

'All hail, my royal sister!' answered Nyelptha. 'Draw thou near. Fear not, I give thee safe conduct.'

Sorais answered with a haughty look, and swept on up the hall till she stood right before the thrones.

'A boon, oh Queen!' she cried again.

'Speak on, my sister; what is there that I can give thee who hath half our kingdom?'

'Thou canst tell me a true word – me and the people of Zu-Vendis. Art thou, or art thou not, about to take this foreign wolf,' and she pointed to Sir Henry with her toy spear, 'to be a husband to thee, and share thy bed and throne?'

Up Nyleptha rose and, descending from the throne, swept in all the glory of her royal grace on to where her lover stood. There she stopped and untwined the golden snake that was wound around her arm. Then she bade him kneel, and he dropped on one knee on the marble before her, and next, taking the golden snake with both her hands, she bent the pure soft metal round his neck, and when it was fast, deliberately kissed him on the brow and called him her 'dear lord'.

'Thou seest,' she said, when the excited murmur of the spectators had died away, addressing her sister as Sir Henry rose to his feet, 'I have put my collar round the "wolf's" neck, and behold! he shall be my watchdog, and that is my answer to thee, Queen Sorais, my sister, and to those with thee.'

Then, turning to the audience, she continued in a clear proud tone, 'Ay, Lady of the Night, Lords, Priests, and People here gathered together, by this sign do I take the foreigner to husband, even here in the face of you all.' And she took his hand and gazed proudly on him. It was a bold stroke for her to make, and it appealed to the imagination; but human nature in Zu-Vendis, as elsewhere, loves that which is bold and not afraid to break a rule, and is moreover peculiarly susceptible to appeals to its poetical side.

And so the people cheered till the roof rang; but Sorais of the Night stood there with downcast eyes, for she could not bear to see her sister's triumph.

She lifted her white face, the teeth were set, and there were purple rings beneath her glowing eyes. Thrice she tried to speak and thrice she failed, but at last her voice came. Raising her silver spear, she shook it, and the light glanced from it and from the golden scales of her cuirass.

'And thinkest thou, Nyleptha,' she said in notes which pealed through the great hall like a clarion, 'thinkest thou that I, Sorais, a Queen of the Zu-Vendi, will brook that this base outlander shall sit upon my father's throne and rear up half-breeds to fill the place of the great House of the Stairway? Never! never! while there is life in my bosom and a man to follow me and a spear to strike with. Now hand thou over this foreign wolf and those who came hither to prey with him to the doom of fire, for have they not committed the deadly sin against the Sun? or, Nyleptha, I give thee War – red War! And I tell ye strangers – all save thou Bougwan, whom because thou didst do me a service I will save alive if thou wilt leave these men and follow me' (here poor Good shook his head vigorously and ejaculated 'Can't be done' in English) – 'that I will wrap you in sheets of gold and hang you yet alive in chains from the four golden trumpets of the four angels that fly east and west and north and south from the giddiest pinnacles of the Temple, so that ye may be a token and a warning to the land. And as for thee, Incubu, thou shalt die in yet another fashion that I will not tell thee now.'

She ceased, panting for breath, for her passion shook her like a storm, and a murmur, partly of horror and partly of admiration, ran through the hall. Then Nyleptha answered calmly and with dignity: 'Ill would it become my place and dignity, oh sister, so to speak as thou hast spoken and so to threat as thou hast threatened. Yet if thou wilt make war, then will I strive to bear up against thee. Thou, who but yesterday didst strive to win my lover and my lord from me, whom to-day thou dost call a "foreign wolf", to be *thy* lover and *thy* lord' (here there was an immense sensation in the hall), 'thou who but last night, didst creep like a snake into my sleeping-place – ay, even by a secret way, and wouldst have foully murdered me, thy sister, as I lay asleep—'

'It is false, it is false!' rang out Agon's and a score of other voices.

'It is *not* false,' said I, producing the broken point of the dagger and holding it up. 'Where is the haft from which this flew, oh Sorais?'

'It is not false,' cried Good, determined at last to act like a loyal man. 'I took the Lady of the Night by the White Queen's bed, and on my breast the dagger broke.'

'Who is on my side?' cried Sorais, shaking her silver spear, for she saw that public sympathy was turning against her. 'What, Bougwan, thou comest not?' she said, addressing Good, who was standing close to her, in a low, concentrated voice. 'Thou pale-souled fool, for a reward thou shalt eat out thy heart with love of me and not be satisfied, and thou mightest have been my husband and a king! At least I hold *thee* in chains that cannot be broken.

'*War! War! War!*' she cried. 'Who follows Sorais of the Night to victory and honour?'

Instantly the whole concourse began to break up in indescribable confusion. Many present hastened to throw in their lot with the 'Lady of the Night', but some came from her following to us.

'Shut the gates,' I shouted, thinking that we might perhaps catch Sorais so, and not being troubled with the idea of committing sacrilege. But the order came too late, her guards were already passing through them, and in another minute the streets echoed with the furious galloping of horses and the rolling of her chariots.

So, drawing half the people after her, Sorais was soon passing like a whirlwind through the Frowning City on her road to her headquarters at M'Arstuna, a fortress situated a hundred and thirty miles to the north of Milosis.

And after that the city was alive with the endless tramp of regiments and preparations for the gathering war, and old Umslopogaas once more began to sit in the sunshine and go through a show of sharpening Inkosi-kaas's razor edge.

EIGHTEEN

A Strange Wedding

One person, however, did not succeed in getting out in time before the gates were shut, and that was the high priest Agon, who, as we had every reason to believe, was Sorais' great ally, and the heart and soul of her party. This cunning and ferocious old man had not forgiven us for those hippo-potami, or rather that was what he said. What he meant was that he would never brook the introduction of our wider ways of thought and foreign learning and influence while there was a possibility of stamping us out.

When we knew that Agon was caught, Nyleptha, Sir Henry, and I discussed what was to be done with him. I was for closely incarcerating him, but Nyleptha shook her head, saying that it would produce a disastrous effect throughout the country. 'Ah!' she added, with a stamp of her foot, 'if I win and am once really Queen, I will break the power of those priests, with their rites and revels and dark secret ways.' I only wished that old Agon could have heard her, it would have frightened him.

'Well,' said Sir Henry, 'if we are not to imprison him, I

suppose that we may as well let him go. He is of no use here.'

Nyleptha looked at him in a curious sort of way, and said in a dry little voice, 'Thinkest thou so, my lord?'

'Eh?' said Curtis. 'No, I do not see what is the use of keeping him.'

She said nothing, but continued looking at him in a way that was as shy as it was sweet.

Then at last he understood.

'Forgive me, Nyleptha,' he said rather tremulously. 'Dost thou mean that thou wilt marry me, even now?'

'Nay, I know not; let my lord say,' was her rapid answer; 'but if my lord wills, the priest is there and the altar is there' – pointing to the entrance to a private chapel – 'and am I not ready to do the will of my lord? Listen, oh my lord! in eight days or less thou must leave me and go down to war, for thou shalt lead my armies, and in war men sometimes fall, and if so I would for a little space have had thee all my own, if only for memory's sake;' and the tears overflowed her lovely eyes.

I left then and went back to our quarters and ruminated over things in general, and watched old Umslopogaas whetting his axe outside the window as a vulture whets his beak beside a dying ox.

And in about an hour's time Sir Henry came tearing over, looking very radiant and wildly excited, and found Good and myself and even Umslopogaas, and asked us if we should like to assist at a real wedding. Of course we said yes, and off we went to the chapel, where we found Agon looking as sulky as any high priest possibly could. He had flatly refused to celebrate the wedding or to allow any of his priests to do so, whereupon Nyleptha became very angry and told him that she, as Queen, was head of the Church, and meant to be obeyed.

So it chanced that presently, attended only by two of her favourite maidens, came the Queen Nyleptha, with happy blushing face and downcast eyes, dressed in pure white. She did not wear a single ornament, and I thought that if possible she looked more lovely than ever without them, as really superbly beautiful women do.

She came, curtseyed low to Sir Henry, and then took his hand and led him up before the altar, and after a little pause, in a slow, clear voice uttered the following words, which are customary in Zu-Vendis if the bride desires and the man consents: –

'Thou dost swear by the Sun that thou wilt take no other woman to wife unless I lay my hand upon her and bid her come?'

'I swear it,' answered Sir Henry; adding in English, 'One is quite enough for me.'

Then Agon, who had been sulking in a corner near the altar, came forward and gabbled off something into his beard at such a rate that I could not follow it, but it appeared to be an invocation to the Sun to bless the union and make it fruitful.

At the end of the invocations they were asked, as in our service, if they took each other for husband and wife, and on their assenting they kissed each other before the altar, and the service was over, so far as their rites were concerned. But it seemed to me that there was yet something wanting and so I produced a Prayer-Book.

'Curtis,' I said, 'I am not a clergyman, and I do not know if what I am going to propose is allowable – I know it is not legal – but if you and the Queen have no objection I should like to read the English marriage service over you. It is a solemn step which you are taking, and I think that you ought, so far as circumstances will allow, to give it the sanction of your own religion.'

'I have thought of that,' he said, 'and I wish you would. I do not feel half married yet.'

Nyleptha raised no objection, fully understanding that

her husband wished to celebrate the marriage according to the rites prevailing in his own country, and so I set to work and read the service.

Then Sir Henry took a plain gold ring from his little finger and placed it on hers.

As for Agon, he was with difficulty kept calm while this second ceremony was going on, for he at once set me down as a rival High Priest, and hated me accordingly. However, in the end off he went, positively bristling with indignation, and I knew that we might look out for danger from his direction.

And off went Good and I, and old Umslopogaas also, leaving the happy pair to themselves.

Good and I went and ate in silence and then indulged in an extra fine flagon of old Zu-Vendian wine, and presently one of our attendants came and told a story that gave us something to think about.

It seemed that Alphonse had gone for a walk in the pleasure gardens. After wandering about there for a little he started to return, but was met near the outer gate by Sorais' train of chariots, which were galloping furiously along the great northern road. When she caught sight of Alphonse, Sorais halted her train and called to him. On approaching he was instantly seized and dragged into one of the chariots and carried off, 'crying out loudly', as our informant said, and as from my general knowledge of him I can well believe.

At first I was much puzzled to know what object Sorais could have had in carrying off the poor little Frenchman. Then an idea occurred to me. We three were, as I think I have said, much revered by the people of Zu-Vendis at large, both because we were the first strangers they had ever seen, and because we were supposed to be the possessors of almost supernatural wisdom. The outcry against us was to a considerable extent fictitious, and nobody knew it better than Sorais herself. Consequently it struck me that it might have occurred to her that it would be better to place the reason of her conflict with her sister upon other and more general grounds than Nyleptha's marriage with the stranger. This being so, it was of great importance to her to have one of the strangers with her whom she could show to the common people as a great Outlander, who had been so struck by the justice of her cause that he had elected to follow her.

This no doubt was the cause of her anxiety to get a hold of Good, whom she would have used till he ceased to be of service and then cast off. But Good having drawn back she grasped at the opportunity of securing Alphonse, who was not unlike him in personal appearance though smaller, no doubt with the object of showing him off in the cities and country as the great Bougwan himself. I told Good that I thought that that was her plan, and his face was a sight to see – he was so horrified at the idea.

Well, that night Good and I dined as I have said in solitary grandeur. Next morning the work began in good earnest. The messages and orders which had been despatched by Nyleptha two days before now began to take effect, and multitudes of armed men came pouring into the city. We saw, as may be imagined, but very little of Nyleptha and not too much of Curtis during those next few days, but Good and I sat daily with the council of generals and loyal lords, drawing up plans of action, arranging commissariat matters, the distribution of commands, and a hundred and one other things. Men came in freely, and all the day long the great roads leading to Milosis were spotted with the banners of lords arriving from their distant places to rally round Nyleptha.

After the first two days it became clear that we should be able to take the field with about forty thousand infantry and twenty thousand cavalry. But if our force was large, Sorais' was, according to the reports brought in day by day by our spies, much larger. She had taken up her headquarters at a very strong town called M'Arstuna, situated, as I have said, to the north of Milosis, and all the countryside was flocking to her standard. Nasta had poured down from his highlands and was on his way to join her with no less than twenty-five thousand of his mountaineers, the most terrible soldiers to face in all Zu-Vendis. Another mighty lord, named Belusha, who lived in the great horse-breeding district, had come in with twelve thousand cavalry, and so on. It seemed certain that she would gather a fully armed host of nearly one hundred thousand men.

And then came news that Sorais was proposing to break up her camp and march on the Frowning City itself, desolating the country as she came. Thereon arose the question whether it would be best to meet her at Milosis or to go out and give her battle. When our opinion was asked upon the subject, Good and I unhesitatingly gave it in favour of an advance. We cast our vote for moving out and giving battle in the open, instead of waiting till we were drawn from our walls like a badger from a hole.

Sir Henry's opinion coincided with ours, and so, needless to say, did that of Nyleptha, who, like a flint, was always ready to flash out fire. A great map of the country was brought and spread out before her. About thirty miles this side of M'Arstuna, where Sorais lay, and ninety odd miles from Milosis, the road ran over a neck of land some two and a half miles in width, and flanked on either side by forest-clad hills which, without being lofty, would, if the road were blocked, be quite impracticable for a great baggage-laden army to cross. She looked earnestly at the map, and then she laid her finger upon this neck of rising ground, and turning to her husband, said, with a proud air of confidence and a toss of the golden head –

'Here shalt thou meet Sorais' armies. I know the spot, here shalt thou meet them, and drive them before thee like dust before the storm.'

But Curtis looked grave and said nothing.

NINETEEN

The Battle of the Pass

It was on the third morning after this incident of the map that Sir Henry and I started. With the exception of a small guard, all the great host had moved on the night before, leaving the Frowning City very silent and empty. Indeed, it was found impossible to leave any garrison with the exception of a personal guard for Nyleptha, and about a thousand men who from sickness or one cause or another were unable to proceed with the army; but as Milosis was practically impregnable, and as our enemy was in front of and not behind us, this did not so much matter.

Good and Umslopogaas had gone on with the army, but Nyleptha accompanied Sir Henry and myself to the city gates, riding a magnificent white horse called Daylight, which was supposed to be the fleetest and most enduring animal in Zu-Vendis. Her face bore traces of recent weeping, but there were no tears in her eyes now, indeed she was bearing up bravely against what must have been a bitter trial to her. At the gate she reined in her horse and bade us farewell.

'Fare thee well, Macumazahn!' she said. 'Remember, I

trust to thy wits, which are as a needle to a spear-handle compared to those of my people, to save us from Sorais. I know that thou wilt do thy duty.'

She turned to Curtis.

'Fare thee well, my lord!' she said. 'Come back with victory, and as a king, or on thy soldiers' spears.'

Sir Henry said nothing, but turned his horse to go; perhaps he had a bit of a lump in his throat. One gets over it afterwards, but these sort of partings are trying when one has only been married a week.

'Here,' added Nyleptha, 'will I greet ye when ye return in triumph. And now, my lords, once more, farewell!'

Then we rode on, but when we had gone a hundred and fifty yards or so, we turned and perceived her still sitting on her horse at the same spot, and looking out after us beneath her hand, and that was the last we saw of her. About a mile farther on, however, we heard galloping behind us, and looking round, saw a mounted soldier coming towards us, leading Nyleptha's matchless steed – Daylight.

'The Queen sends the white stallion as a farewell gift to her Lord Incubu, and bids me tell my lord that he is the fleetest and the most enduring horse in all the land,' said the soldier, bending to his saddle-bow before us.

Then we marched on without meeting with any opposition, almost indeed without seeing anybody, for the populations of the towns and villages along our route had for the most part fled, fearing lest they should be caught between the two rival armies and ground to powder like grain between the upper and the nether stones.

On the evening of the fourth day, for the progress of so great a multitude was necessarily slow, we camped two miles this side of the neck or ridge I have spoken of, and our outposts brought us word that Sorais with all her power was rolling down upon us, and had pitched her camp that night ten miles the farther side of the neck.

Accordingly before dawn we sent forward fifteen hundred cavalry to seize the position. Scarcely had they occupied it, however, before they were attacked by about as many of Sorais' horsemen, and a very smart little cavalry fight ensued, with a loss to us of about thirty men killed. On the advance of our supports, however, Sorais' force drew off, carrying their dead and wounded with them.

The main body of the army reached the neck about dinner-time, and I must say that Nyleptha's judgment had not failed her, it was an admirable place to give battle in, especially to a superior force.

The road ran down a mile or more, through ground too broken to admit of the handling of any considerable force, till it reached the crest of a great green wave of land, that rolled down a gentle slope to the banks of a little stream, and then rolled away again up a still gentler slope to the plain beyond, the distance from the crest of the land-wave down to the stream being a little over half a mile, and from the stream up to the plain beyond a trifle less. The length of this wave of land at its highest point, which corresponded exactly with the width of the neck of land between the wooded hills, was about two miles and a quarter, and it was protected on either side by dense, rocky, bush-clad ground, that afforded a most valuable cover to the flanks of the army and rendered it almost impossible for them to be turned.

It was on the hither slope of this neck of land that Curtis encamped his army. Our force of sixty thousand men was, roughly speaking, divided as follows. In the centre was a dense body of twenty thousand foot-soldiers, armed with spears, swords, and hippopotamus-hide shields, breast and back plates. These formed the chest of the army, and were supported by five thousand foot, and three thousand horse in reserve. On either side of this chest were stationed seven thousand horse arranged in deep, majestic squadrons; and beyond and on either side but slightly in front of them again were two bodies, each numbering about seven thousand five hundred spearmen, forming the right and left wings of the army, and each supported by a contingent of some fifteen hundred cavalry.

Curtis commanded in chief, I was in command of the seven thousand horse between the chest and right wing, which was commanded by Good, and the other battalions and squadrons were entrusted to Zu-Vendi generals.

Scarcely had we taken up our positions before Sorais' vast army began to swarm on the opposite slope about a mile in front of us, till the whole place seemed alive with the multitude of her spear-points, and the ground shook with the tramp of her battalions. It was evident that the spies had not exaggerated; we were outnumbered by at least a third. At first we expected that Sorais was going to attack us at once, as the clouds of cavalry which hung upon her flanks executed some threatening demonstrations, but she thought better of it, and there was no fight that day.

Opposite our right wing, and forming Sorais' left wing, was a great army of dark, wild-looking men, armed with sword and shield only, which, I was informed, was composed of Nasta's twenty-five thousand savage hillsmen.

All day we watched and waited, but nothing happened, and at last night fell, and a thousand watch-fires twinkled brightly on the slopes, to wane and die one by one like the stars they resembled. As the hours wore on, the silence gradually gathered more deeply over the opposing hosts. Deep into the night we sat, with pale faces and heavy hearts, and took counsel, whilst the sentries tramped up and down, down and up, and the armed and plumed generals came and went, grim and shadow-like.

And so the time wore away, till everything was ready for the coming slaughter; and I lay down and thought, and tried to get a little rest, but could not sleep for fear of the morrow – for who could say what the morrow would bring forth?

Misery and death, this was certain; beyond that we knew not, and I confess I was very much afraid.

And at last up came the red sun, and the huge camps awoke with a clash, and a roar, and gathered themselves together for battle. It was a beautiful and awe-inspiring scene, and old Umslopogaas, leaning on his axe, contemplated it with grim delight.

'Never have I seen the like, Macumazahn, never,' he said. 'The battles of my people are as the play of children to what this will be. Thinkest thou that they will fight it out?'

'Ay,' I answered sadly, 'to the death. Content thyself, "Woodpecker", for once shalt thou peck thy fill.'

Time went on, and still there was no sign of an attack.

About midday, when the men were eating their dinner, for we thought they would fight better on full stomachs, a shout of '*Sorais, Sorais*', arose like thunder from the enemy's extreme right, and taking the glass, I was able to clearly distinguish the 'Lady of the Night', herself, surrounded by a glittering staff, and riding slowly down the lines of her battalions. And as she went, that mighty, thundering shout rolled along before her like the rolling of ten thousand chariots, or the roaring of the ocean when the gale turns suddenly and carries the noise of it to the listeners' ears, till the earth shook, and the air was full of the majesty of sound.

We had not long to wait. Suddenly, like flame from a cannon's mouth, out shot two great tongue-like forces of cavalry, and came charging down the slope towards the little stream, slowly at first, but gathering speed as they came. Before they got to the stream, orders reached me from Sir Henry, who evidently feared that the shock of such a charge, if allowed to fall unbroken upon our infantry, would be too much for them, to send five thousand sabres to meet the force opposite to me, at the moment when it began to mount the stiffest of the rise about four hundred yards from our lines. This I did, remaining behind myself with the rest of my men.

Off went a general with five thousand horsemen, drawn up in a wedge-like form. Starting at a hand gallop, for the first three hundred yards he rode straight at the tip of the tongue-shaped mass of cavalry which, numbering, so far as I could judge, about eight thousand sabres, was advancing to charge us. Then he suddenly swerved to the right and put on the pace, and I saw the great wedge curl round, and before the foe could check himself and turn to meet it, strike him about halfway down his length, with a crashing rending sound, like that of the breaking-up of vast sheets of ice. In sank the great wedge, into his heart, and as it cut its way hundreds of horsemen were thrown up on either side of it. Still farther in, by Heaven! right through, and so, amid cheer after cheer from our watching thousands, back again upon the severed ends, beating them down, driving them as a gale drives spray, till at last, amidst the rushing of hundreds of riderless horses, the flashing of swords, and the victorious clamour of their pursuers, the great force crumples up like an empty glove, then turns and gallops pell-mell for safety back to its own lines.

I do not think it reached them more than two-thirds as strong as it went out ten minutes before. The lines which were now advancing to the attack, opened and swallowed them up, and my force returned, having only suffered a loss of about five hundred men – not much, I thought, considering the fierceness of the struggle.

By this time the dense masses of the enemy's left, composed almost entirely of Nasta's swordsmen, were across the little stream, and with alternate yells of 'Nasta' and 'Sorais', with dancing banners and gleaming swords, were swarming up towards us like ants.

Again I received orders to try and check this movement, and also the main advance against the chest of our army, by means of cavalry charges, and this I did to the best of my ability, by continually sending squadrons of about a thousand sabres out against them. These squadrons did the enemy much damage, and it was a glorious sight to see them flash down the hill-side, and bury themselves like a living knife in the heart of the foe. But, also, we lost many men, for after the experience of a couple of these charges, which had drawn a sort of blood St Andrew's cross of dead and dying through the centre of Nasta's host, our foes no longer attempted to offer an unyielding front to their irresistible weight, but opened out to let the rush go through, throwing themselves on the ground and hamstringing hundreds of horses as they passed.

And so, notwithstanding all that we could do, the enemy drew nearer, till at last he hurled himself upon Good's force of seven thousand five hundred regulars, who were drawn up to receive them in three strong squares. About the same time, too, an awful and heartshaking roar told me that the main battle had closed in on the centre and extreme left. I raised myself in my stirrups and looked down to my left; so far as the eye could see there was a long dazzling shimmer of steel as the sun glanced upon falling sword and thrusting spear.

To and fro swung the contending lines in that dread struggle, now giving way, now gaining a little in the mad yet ordered confusion of attack and defence.

Nasta's wild swordsmen were now breaking in red waves against the sullen rock-like squares. Time after time did they yell out their war-cries, and hurl themselves furiously against the long triple ridges of spear points, only to be rolled back as billows are when they meet the cliff.

And so for four long hours the battle raged almost without a pause, and at the end of that time, if we had gained nothing we had lost nothing.

As for the chest of the army where Sir Henry was with his staff and Umslopogaas, it had suffered dreadfully, but it had held its own with honour, and the same may be said of our left battle.

At last the attacks slackened, and Sorais' army drew back, having, I began to think, had enough of it. On this point, however, I was soon undeceived, for splitting up her cavalry into comparatively small squadrons, she charged us furiously with them, all along the line, and then once more sullenly rolled her tens of thousands of sword and spearmen down upon our weakened squares and squadrons; Sorais herself directing the movement, and fearless as a lioness heading the main attack. On they came like an avalanche – I saw her golden helm gleaming in the van – our counter charges of cavalry entirely failing to check their forward sweep. Now they had struck us, and our centre bent in like a bow beneath the weight of their rush – it parted, and had not the ten thousand men in reserve charged down to its support it must have been utterly destroyed. As for Good's three squares, they were swept backwards like boats upon an incoming tide, and the foremost one was burst into and lost half its remaining men. But the effort was too fierce and terrible to last. Suddenly the battle came, as it were, to a turning-point, and for a minute or two stood still.

Then it began to move towards Sorais' camp. Just then, too, Nasta's fierce and almost invincible highlanders, either because they were disheartened by their losses or by way of a ruse, fell back, and the remains of Good's gallant squares, leaving the positions they had held for so many hours, cheered wildly, and rashly followed them down the slope, whereon the swarms of swordsmen turned to envelop them, and once more flung themselves upon them with a yell. Taken thus on every side, what remained of the first square was quickly destroyed, and I perceived that the second, in which I could see Good himself mounted on a large horse, was on the point of annihilation. A few more minutes and it was broken, its streaming colours sank, and I lost sight of

Good in the confused and hideous slaughter that ensued.

Presently, however, a cream-coloured horse with a snow-white mane and tail burst from the ruins of the square and came rushing past me riderless and with wide streaming reins, and in it I recognized the charger that Good had been riding. Then I hesitated no longer, but taking with me half my effective cavalry force, which now amounted to between four and five thousand men, I commended myself to God, and, without waiting for orders, I charged straight down upon Nasta's swordsmen. Seeing me coming, and being warned by the thunder of my horses' hoofs, the majority of them faced round, and gave us a right warm welcome. Not an inch would they yield; in vain did we hack and trample them down as we ploughed a broad red furrow through their thousands; they seemed to re-arise by hundreds, driving their terrible sharp swords into our horses, or severing their hamstrings, and then hacking the troopers who came to the ground with them almost into pieces. My horse was speedily killed under me, but luckily I had a fresh one, my own favourite, a coal-black mare Nyleptha had given me, being held in reserve behind, and on this I afterwards mounted. Meanwhile I had to get along as best I could, for I was pretty well lost sight of by my men in the mad confusion of the moment. My voice, of course, could not be heard in the midst of the clanging of steel and the shrieks of rage and agony. Presently I found myself mixed up with the remnants of the square, which had formed round its leader Good, and was fighting desperately for existence. I stumbled against somebody, and glancing down, caught sight of Good's eyeglass. He had been beaten to his knee. Over him was a great fellow swinging a heavy sword. Somehow I managed to run the man through with the sime I had taken from the Masai whose hand I had cut off; but as I did so, he dealt me a frightful blow on the left side and breast with the sword, and though my chain shirt

saved my life, I felt that I was badly hurt. For a minute I fell
on to my hands and knees among the dead and dying, and
turned sick and faint. When I came to again I saw that
Nasta's spearmen, or rather those of them who remained,
were retreating back across the stream, and that Good was
there by me smiling sweetly.

'Near go that,' he shouted; 'but all's well that ends well.'

I assented, but I could not help feeling that it had not
ended well for me. I was sorely hurt.

Just then we saw the smaller bodies of cavalry stationed
on our extreme right and left, and which were now re-
inforced by the three thousand sabres which we had held in
reserve, flash out like arrows from their posts and fall upon
the disordered flanks of Sorais' forces, and that charge
decided the issue of the battle. In another minute or two the
enemy was in slow and sullen retreat across the little stream,
where they once more reformed. Then came another lull,
during which I managed to get my second horse, and received my orders to advance from Sir Henry, and then with
one fierce deep-throated roar, with a waving of banners and a
wide flashing of steel, the remains of our army took the
offensive and began to sweep down, slowly indeed, but irre-
sistibly from the positions they had so gallantly held all day.

At last it was our turn to attack.

On we moved, over the piled-up masses of dead and
dying, and were approaching the stream, when suddenly I
perceived an extraordinary sight. Galloping wildly towards
us, his arms tightly clasped around his horse's neck, against
which his blanched cheek was tightly pressed, was a man
arrayed in the full costume of a Zu-Vendi general, but in
whom, as he came nearer, I recognized none other than our
lost Alphonse. It was impossible even then to mistake those
curling black mustachios. In a minute he was tearing
through our ranks and narrowly escaped being cut down,
till at last somebody caught his horse's bridle, and he was

brought to me just as a momentary halt occurred in our
advance to allow what remained of our shattered squares to
form into line.

'Ah, monsieur,' he gasped out in a voice that was nearly
inarticulate with fright, 'grace to the sky, it is you! Ah, what
I have endured! But you win, monsieur, you win; they fly,
the laches. But listen, monsieur – I forget, it is no good; the
Queen is to be murdered to-morrow at the first light in the
palace of Milosis; her guards will leave their posts, and
the priests are going to kill her. Ah yes! they little thought
it, but I was ensconced beneath a banner, and I heard it all.'

'What?' I said, horror-struck; 'what do you mean?'

'What I say, monsieur; that devil of a Nasta he went last
night to settle the affair with the Archbishop [Agon]. The
guard will leave open the little gate leading from the great
stair and go away, and Nasta and Agon's priests will come in
and kill her. Themselves they would not kill her.'

'Come with me,' I said, and, shouting to the staff-officer
next to me to take over the command, I snatched his bridle and
galloped as hard as I could for the spot, between a quarter
and half a mile off, where I saw the royal pennon flying, and
where I knew that I should find Curtis if he were still alive.
On we tore, our horses clearing heaps of dead and dying
men, and splashing through pools of blood, on past the long
broken lines of spearmen to where, mounted on the white
stallion Nyleptha had sent to him as a parting gift, I saw Sir
Henry's form towering above the generals who surrounded
him.

Just as we reached him the advance began again. A
bloody cloth was bound around his head, but I saw that his
eye was as bright and keen as ever. Beside him was old
Umslopogaas, his axe red with blood, but looking quite
fresh and uninjured.

'What's wrong, Quatermain?' he shouted.

'Everything. There is a plot to murder the Queen to-morrow at dawn. Alphonse here, who has just escaped from Sorais, has overheard it all,' and I rapidly repeated to him what the Frenchman had told me.

Curtis' face turned deadly pale and his jaw dropped.

'At dawn,' he gasped, 'and it is now sunset; it dawns before four and we are nearly a hundred miles off – nine hours at the outside. What is to be done?'

An idea entered into my head. 'Is that horse of yours fresh?' I said.

'Yes, I have only just got on to him – when my last was killed, and he has been fed.'

'So is mine. Get off him, and let Umslopogaas mount; he can ride well. We will be at Milosis before dawn, or if we are not – well, we cannot help it. No, no; it is impossible for you to leave now. You would be seen, and it would turn the fate of the battle. It is not half won yet. The soldiers would think you were making a bolt of it. Quick now.'

In a moment he was down, and at my bidding Umslopogaas sprang into the empty saddle.

'Now farewell,' I said. 'Send a thousand horsemen with remounts after us in an hour if possible. Stay, despatch a general to the left wing to take over the command and explain my absence.'

'You will do your best to save her, Quatermain?' he said in a broken voice.

'Ay, that I will. Go on; you are being left behind.'

He cast one glance at us, and accompanied by his staff galloped off to join the advance, which by this time was fording the little brook that now ran red with the blood of the fallen.

As for Umslopogaas and myself, we left that dreadful field as arrows leave a bow, and in a few minutes had passed right out of the sight of slaughter, the smell of blood, and the turmoil and shouting, which only came to our ears as a faint, far-off roaring like the sound of distant breakers.

TWENTY
Away! Away!

At the top of the rise we halted for a second to breathe our horses; and, turning, glanced at the battle beneath us, which, illumined as it was by the fierce rays of the sinking sun staining the whole scene red, looked from where we were more like some wild titanic picture than an actual hand-to-hand combat. The distinguishing scenic effect from that distance was the countless distinct flashes of light reflected from the swords and spears.

'We win the day, Macumazahn,' said old Umslopogaas, taking in the whole situation with a glance of his practised eye. 'Look, the Lady of the Night's forces give on every side, there is no stiffness left in them, they bend like hot iron, they are fighting with but half a heart. But alas! the battle will in a manner be drawn, for the darkness gathers, and the regiments will not be able to follow and slay!' – and he shook his head sadly. 'But,' he added, 'I do not think that they will fight again, we have fed them with too strong a meat. Ah! it is well to have lived! At last I have seen a fight worth seeing.'

By this time we were on our way again, and as we went side by side I told him what our mission was, and how that, if it failed, all the lives that had been lost that day would have been lost in vain.

'Ah!' he said, 'nigh on a hundred miles and no horses but these, and to be there before the dawn! Well – away! away! man can but try, Macumazahn; and mayhap we shall be there in time to split that old "witch-finder's" [Agon's] skull for him." And he shook Inkosi-kaas as he galloped. By now the darkness was closing in, but fortunately there would be a moon later, and the road was good.

On we sped through the twilight, the two splendid horses we bestrode had got their wind by this time, and were sweeping along with a wide steady stride that neither failed nor varied for mile upon mile. Down the sides of slopes we galloped, across wide vales that stretched to the foot of far-off hills. Nearer and nearer grew the blue hills; now we were travelling up their steeps, and now we were over and passing towards others that sprang up like visions in the far, faint distance beyond.

On, never pausing or drawing rein, through the perfect quiet of the night, that was set like a song to the falling music of our horses' hooves; on, past deserted villages, where only some forgotten starving dog howled a melancholy welcome; on, past lonely moated dwellings; on, through the white patchy moonlight, that lay coldly upon the wide bosom of the earth, as though there was no warmth in it; on, knee to knee, for hour after hour!

We spake not, but bent us forward on the necks of those two glorious horses, and listened to their deep, long-drawn breaths as they filled their great lungs, and to the regular unfaltering ring of their round hoofs.

And so on, still on, without break or pause for hour after hour.

At last I felt that even the splendid animal that I rode was

beginning to give out. I looked at my watch; it was nearly
midnight, and we were considerably more than half way.
On the top of a rise was a little spring, which I remembered
because I had slept by it a few nights before, and here I
motioned to Umslopogaas to pull up, having determined to
give the horses and ourselves ten minutes to breathe in. He
did so, and we dismounted – that is to say, Umslopogaas
did, and then helped me off, for what with fatigue, stiffness,
and the pain of my wound, I could not do so for myself; and
the gallant horses stood panting there, resting first one leg
and then another, while the sweat fell drip, drip, from
them, and the steam rose and hung in pale clouds in the still
night air.

Leaving Umslopogaas to hold the horses, I hobbled to the
spring and drank deep of its sweet waters. I had had nothing
but a single mouthful of wine since midday, when the battle
began, and I was parched up, though my fatigue was too
great to allow me to feel hungry. Then, having laved my
fevered head and hands, I returned, and the Zulu went and
drank. Next we allowed the horses to take a couple of
mouthfuls each – no more; and oh, what a struggle we had
to get the poor beasts away from the water! There were yet
two minutes, and I employed it in hobbling up and down to
try and relieve my stiffness, and in inspecting the condition
of the horses. My mare, gallant animal though she was, was
evidently much distressed; she hung her head, and her eye
looked sick and dull; but Daylight, Nyleptha's glorious
horse was still comparatively speaking fresh, notwithstanding that he had had by far the heavier weight to carry. He
was 'tucked up', indeed, and his legs were weary, but his
eye was bright and clear, and he held his shapely head up
and gazed out into the darkness round him in a way that
seemed to say that whoever failed *he* was good for those
five-and-forty miles that yet lay between us and Milosis.
Then Umslopogaas helped me into the saddle and vaulted

into his own without touching a stirrup, and we were off
once more, slowly at first, till the horses got into their stride,
and then more swiftly. So we passed over another ten miles,
and then came a long, weary ride of some six or seven miles,
and three times did my poor black mare nearly come to the
ground with me. But on the top she seemed to gather herself
together, and rattled down the slope with long, convulsive
strides, breathing in gasps. We did that three or four miles
more swiftly than any since we had started on our wild ride,
but I felt it to be a last effort, and I was right. Suddenly my
poor horse took the bit between her teeth and bolted
furiously along a stretch of level ground for some three or
four hundred yards, and then, with two or three jerky
strides, pulled herself up and fell with a crash right on to her
head, I rolling myself free as she did so. As I struggled on
to my feet the brave beast raised her head and looked at
me with piteous bloodshot eyes, and then her head
dropped with a groan and she was dead. Her heart was
broken.

Umslopogaas pulled up beside the carcase, and I looked
at him in dismay. There were still more than twenty miles to
do by dawn, and how were we to do it with one horse? It
seemed hopeless, but I had forgotten the old Zulu's extraordinary running powers.

Without a single word he sprang from the saddle and
began to hoist me into it.

'What wilt thou do?' I asked.

'Run,' he answered, seizing my stirrup-leather.

Then off we went again, almost as fast as before; and oh,
the relief it was to me to get that change of horses! Anybody
who has ever ridden against time will know what it meant.

Daylight sped along at a long stretching hand-gallop,
giving the gaunt Zulu a lift at every stride. It was a
wonderful thing to see old Umslopogaas run mile after mile,
his lips slightly parted and his nostrils agape like the

horse's. Every five miles or so we stopped for a few minutes to let him get his breath, and then flew on again.

'Canst thou go farther,' I said at the third of these stoppages, 'or shall I leave thee to follow me?'

He pointed with his axe to a dim mass before us. It was the Temple of the Sun, now not more than five miles away.

'I reach it or I die,' he gasped.

Oh, that last five miles! The skin was rubbed from the inside of my legs, and every movement of my horse gave me anguish. Nor was that all. I was exhausted with toil, want of food and sleep, and also suffering very much from the blow I had received on my left side; it seemed as though a piece of bone or something was slowly piercing into my lung. Poor Daylight, too, was pretty nearly finished, and no wonder. But there was a smell of dawn in the air, and we might not stay; better that all three of us should die upon the road than that we should linger while there was life in us. The air was thick and heavy, as it sometimes is before the dawn breaks.

And now before us are the huge brazen gates of the outer wall of the Frowning City, and a new and horrible doubt strikes me: What if they will not let us in?

'*Open! open!*' I shout imperiously, at the same time giving the royal password. '*Open! open!* a messenger, a messenger with tidings of the war!'

'What news?' cried the guard. 'And who art thou that ridest so madly?'

'It is the Lord Macumazahn. *Open! open!* I bring tidings.'

The great gates ran back on their rollers, and the draw-bridge fell with a rattling crash, and we dashed on through the one and over the other.

'What news, my lord, what news?' cried the guard.

'Incubu rolls Sorais back, as the wind a cloud,' I answered, and was gone.

On, clattering through the sleeping streets.

'Thank God, the palace at last!' and see, the first arrows

of the dawn are striking on the temple's golden dome. But shall I get in here, or is the deed done and the way barred?

Once more I give the password and shout '*Open! open!*'

No answer, and my heart grows very faint.

Again I call, and this time a single voice replies, and to my joy I recognize it as belonging to Kara, a fellow-officer.

'It is thou, Kara?' I cry; 'I am Macumazahn. Bid the guard let down the bridge and throw wide the gate.'

Then followed a space that seemed to me endless, but at length the bridge fell and one half of the gate opened and we got into the courtyard, where at last poor Daylight fell down beneath me, as I thought, dead. I struggled free, and leaning against a post looked around. Except Kara, there was nobody to be seen, and his look was wild, and his garments were all torn.

'Where are the guard?' I gasped, fearing his answer as I never feared anything before.

'I know not,' he answered; 'two hours ago, as I slept, was I seized and bound by the watch under me, and but now, this very moment, have I freed myself with my teeth. I fear, I greatly fear, that we are betrayed.'

His words gave me fresh energy. Catching him by the arm, I staggered, followed by Umslopogaas, who reeled after us like a drunken man, through the courtyards, up the great hall, which was silent as the grave, towards the Queen's sleeping-place.

We reached the first ante-room – no guards; the second, still no guards. Oh, surely the thing was done! we were too late after all, too late! The silence and solitude of those great chambers was dreadful, and weighed me down like an evil dream. On, right into Nyleptha's chamber we rushed and staggered, sick at heart, fearing the very worst; we saw there was a light in it, ay, and a figure bearing the light. Oh, thank God, it is the White Queen herself, the Queen unharmed!

There she stands in her night gear, roused, by the clatter of our coming, from her bed, the heaviness of sleep yet in her eyes, and a red blush of fear and shame mantling her lovely breast and cheek.

'Who is it?' she cries. 'What means this? Oh, Macuma-zahn, is it thou? Why lookest thou so wildly? Thou comest as one bearing evil tidings – and my lord – oh, tell me not my lord is dead – not dead!' she wailed, wringing her white hands.

'I left Incubu wounded, but leading the advance against Sorais last night at sundown; therefore let thy heart have rest. Sorais is beaten back all along her lines, and thy arms prevail.'

'I knew it,' she cried in triumph. 'I knew that he would win; and they called him Outlander, and shook their wise heads when I gave him the command! Last night at sun-down, sayest thou, and it is not yet dawn? Surely—'

'Throw a cloak around thee, Nyleptha,' I broke in, 'and give us wine to drink; ay, and call thy maidens quick if thou wouldst save thyself alive. Nay, stay not.'

Thus adjured she ran and called through the curtains towards some room beyond, and then hastily put on her sandals and a thick cloak, by which time a dozen or so of half-dressed women were pouring into the room.

'Follow us and be silent,' I said to them as they gazed with wondering eyes, clinging one to another. So we went into the first ante-room.

'Now,' I said, 'give us wine to drink and food, if ye have it, for we are near to death.'

The room was used as a mess-room for the officers of the guards, and from a cupboard some flagons of wine and some cold flesh were brought forth, and Umslopogaas and I drank and felt life flow back into our veins as the good red wine went down.

'Hark to me, Nyleptha,' I said, as I put down the empty

tankard. 'Hast thou here among these thy waiting-ladies any two of discretion?'

'Ay,' she said, 'surely.'

'Then bid them go out by the side entrance to any citizens whom thou canst bethink thee of as men loyal to thee and pray them come armed, with all honest folk that they can gather, to rescue thee from death. Nay, question not; do as I say, and quickly. Kara here will let out the maids.'

She turned, and selecting two of the crowd of damsels, repeated the words I had uttered, giving them besides a list of the names of the men to whom each should run.

'Go swiftly and secretly; go for your very lives,' I added.

Though all this takes some time to tell, we had not been but six or seven minutes in the palace; and, notwithstanding that the golden roof of the temple being very lofty was ablaze with the rays of the rising sun, it was not yet dawn, nor would be for another ten minutes. We were in the courtyard now, and here my wound pained me so that I had to take Nyleptha's arm, while Umslopogaas rolled along after us, eating as he went.

Now we were across it, and had reached the narrow doorway through the palace wall that opened on to the mighty stair.

I looked through and stood aghast, as well I might. The door was gone, and so were the outer gates of bronze – entirely gone. They had been taken from their hinges, and as we afterwards found, hurled from the stairway to the ground two hundred feet beneath. There in front of us was the semi-circular standing-space, about twice the size of a large oval dining-table, and the ten curved black marble steps leading on to the main stair – and that was all.

TWENTY-ONE
How Umslopogaas Held the Stair

We looked one at another.

'Thou seest,' I said, 'they have taken away the door. Is there aught with which we may fill the place? Speak quickly, for they will be on us ere the daylight.' I spoke thus, because I knew that we must hold this place or none, as there were no inner doors in the palace, the rooms being separated one from another by curtains. I also knew that if we could by any means defend this doorway the murderers could get in nowhere else; for the palace is absolutely impregnable, that is, since the secret door by which Sorais had entered on that memorable night of attempted murder had, by Nyleptha's order, been closed up with masonry.

'I have it,' said Nyleptha, who, as usual with her, rose to the emergency in a wonderful way. 'On the farther side of the courtyard are blocks of cut marble – the workmen brought them there for the bed of the new statue of Incubu, my lord; let us block the door with them.'

I jumped at the idea; and having despatched one of the remaining maidens down the great stair to see if she could obtain assistance from the docks below, we made our way back across the courtyard to where the hewn marble lay; and here we met Kara returning from despatching the first two messengers. There were the marble blocks, sure enough, broad, massive lumps, some six inches thick, and weighing about eighty pounds each, and there, too, were a couple of implements like small stretchers, that the workmen used to carry them on. Without delay we got some of the blocks on to the stretchers, and four of the girls carried them to the doorway.

'Listen, Macumazahn,' said Umslopogaas, 'if these low fellows come, it is I who will hold the stair against them till the door is build up. Nay, nay, it will be a man's death: gainsay me not, old friend. It has been a good day, let it now be good night. See, I throw myself down to rest on the marble there; when their footsteps are nigh, wake thou me, not before, for I need my strength,' and without a word he went outside and flung himself down on the marble, and was instantly asleep.

At this time, I too was overcome, and was forced to sit down by the doorway, and content myself with directing operations. The girls brought the blocks, while Kara and Nyleptha built them up across the six-foot-wide doorway, a triple row of them, for less would be useless. But the marble had to be brought forty yards, and then there were forty yards to run back, and though the girls laboured gloriously, even staggering along alone, each with a block in her arms, it was slow work, dreadfully slow.

The light was growing now, and presently, in the silence, we heard a commotion at the far-off bottom of the stair, and the faint clanking of armed men. As yet the wall was only two feet high, and we had been eight minutes at the building of it. So they had come. Alphonse had heard aright.

The clanking sound came nearer, and in the ghostly grey of the dawning we could make out long files of men, some fifty or so in all, slowly creeping up the stair. They were now at the half-way standing place that rested on the great flying arch; and there, perceiving that something was going on above, they, to our great gain, halted for three or four minutes and consulted, then slowly and cautiously advanced again.

We had been nearly a quarter of an hour at the work now, and it was almost three feet high.

Then I woke Umslopogaas. The great man rose, stretched himself, and swung Inkosi-kaas round his head.

'It is well,' he said. 'I feel as a young man once more. My strength has come back to me, ay, even as a lamp flares up before it dies. Fear not, I shall fight a good fight; the wine and the sleep have put a new heart into me.' And he took my hand and shook it, and then turned to face the advancing foe.

Just then, to my astonishment, the Zu-Vendi officer Kara clambered over our improvised wall in his quiet, determined sort of way, and took his stand by the Zulu, unsheathing his sword as he did so.

'What, comest thou too?' laughed out the old warrior. 'Welcome – a welcome to thee, brave heart!'

As he spoke, the armed men, among whom in the growing light I recognized both Nasta and Agon, came streaming up the stair with a rush, and one big fellow, armed with a heavy spear, dashed up the ten semicircular steps ahead of his comrades and struck at the great Zulu with the spear. Umslopogaas moved his body but not his legs, so that the blow missed him, and next instant Inkosi-kaas crashed through head-piece, hair and skull, and the man's corpse was rattling down the steps.

In another second the sturdy Kara had also slain a man, and then began a scene the like of which has not been known to me.

Up rushed the assailants, one, two, three at a time, and as

fast as they came, the axe crashed and the sword swung, and down they rolled again, dead or dying. And ever as the fight thickened, the old Zulu's eye seemed to get quicker and his arm stronger. He shouted out his war-cries and the names of chiefs whom he had slain, and the blows of his awful axe rained straight and true, shearing through everything they fell on. There was none of the scientific method he was so fond of about this last immortal fight of his; he had no time for it, but struck with his full strength, and at every stroke a man sank in his tracks, and went rattling down the marble steps.

They hacked and hewed at him with swords and spears, wounding him in a dozen places till he streamed red with blood; but the shield protected his head and the chain-shirt his vitals, and for minute after minute, aided by the gallant Zu-Vendi, he still held the stair.

At last Kara's sword broke, and he grappled with a foe, and they rolled down together, and he was cut to pieces, dying like the brave man that he was.

Umslopogaas was alone now, but he never blenched or turned. Shouting out some wild Zulu battle-cry, he beat down a foe, ay, and another, and another, till at last they drew back from the slippery blood-stained steps, and stared at him in amazement, thinking that he was no mortal man.

The wall of marble block was four feet six high now, and hope rose in my heart as I leaned there against it a miserable helpless log, and ground my teeth, and watched that glorious struggle. I could do no more for I had lost my revolver in the battle.

And old Umslopogaas, he leaned too on his good axe, and, faint as he was with wounds, he mocked them, he called them 'women' – the grand old warrior, standing there one against so many! And for a breathing space none would come against him, notwithstanding Nasta's exhortations, till at last old Agon, who, to do him justice, was a brave man, mad with baffled rage, and seeing that the wall would soon be built and his plans defeated, shook the great spear he held, and rushed up the dripping steps.

'Ah, ah!' shouted the Zulu, as he recognized the priest's flowing white beard, 'it is thou, old "witch-finder!" Come on! I await thee, white "medicine man"; come on! come on! I have sworn to slay thee, and I ever keep my faith.'

On he came, taking him at his word, and drove the big spear with such force at Umslopogaas that it sunk right through the tough shield and pierced him in the neck. The Zulu cast down the transfixed shield, and that moment was Agon's last, for before he could free his spear and strike again, with a shout of *'There's for thee, Rainmaker!'* Umslopogaas gripped Inkosi-kaas with both hands and whirled her on high and drave her right on to his venerable head, so that Agon rolled down dead among the corpses of his fellow-murderers, and there was an end of him and his plots together. And even as he fell, a great cry rose from the foot of the stair, and looking out through the portion of the doorway that was yet unclosed, we saw armed men rushing up to the rescue, and called an answer to their shouts. Then the would-be murderers who yet remained on the stairway, and amongst whom I saw several priests, turned to fly, but, having nowhere to go, were butchered as they fled. Only one man stayed, and he was the great lord Nasta, Nyleptha's suitor, and the father of the plot. For a moment the black-bearded Nasta stood with bowed face leaning on his long sword as though in despair, and then with a dreadful shout, he too rushed up at the Zulu, and, swinging the glittering sword around his head, dealt him such a mighty blow beneath his guard, that the keen steel of the heavy blade bit right through the chain armour and deep into Umslopogaas' side, for a moment paralysing him and causing him to drop his axe.

Raising the sword again, Nasta sprang forward to make

an end of him, but little he knew his foe. With a shake and a yell of fury, the Zulu gathered himself together and sprang straight at Nasta's throat, as I have sometimes seen a wounded lion spring. He struck him full as his foot was on the topmost stair, and his long arms closing round him like iron bands, down they rolled together struggling furiously. Nasta was a strong man and a desperate, but he could not match the strongest man in Zululand, sore wounded though he was, whose strength was as the strength of a bull. In a minute the end came. I saw old Umslopogaas stagger to his feet – ay, and saw him by a single gigantic effort swing up the struggling Nasta and with a shout of triumph hurl him straight over the parapet of the bridge, to be crushed to powder on the rocks two hundred feet below.

The succour which had been summoned by the girl who had passed down the stairs before the assassins passed up was at hand, and the loud shouts which reached us from the outer gates told us that the town was also aroused, and the men awakened by the women were calling to be admitted.

Soon the wall was down again, and through the doorway, followed by a crowd of rescuers, staggered old Umslopogaas, an awful and, in a way, a glorious figure. The man was a mass of wounds, and a glance at his wild eye told me that he was dying. The 'keshla' gum-ring upon his head was severed in two places by sword-cuts, one just over the curious hole in his skull, and the blood poured down his face from the gashes. Also on the right side of his neck was a stab from a spear, inflicted by Agon; there was a deep cut on his left arm just below where the mail shirt-sleeve stopped, and on the right side of his body the armour was severed by a gash six inches long, where Nasta's mighty sword had bitten through it and deep into its wearer's vitals.

On, axe in hand, he staggered, that dreadful-looking, splendid savage. With outstretched arms and tottering gait he pursued his way, followed by us all along the broad shell-strewn walk that ran through the courtyard, past the spot where the blocks of marble lay, through the round arched doorway and the thick curtains that hung within it, down the short passage and into the great hall, which was now filling with hastily-armed men, who poured through the side entrance. Straight up the hall he went, leaving behind him a track of blood on the marble pavement, till at last he reached the sacred stone, which stood in the centre of it, and here his strength seemed to fail him, for he stopped and leaned upon his axe. Then suddenly he lifted up his voice and cried aloud: 'I die, I die – but it was a kingly fray. Where are they who came up the great stair? I see them not. Art thou there, Macumazahn, or art thou gone before to wait for me in the dark whither I go? The blood blinds me – the place turns round – I hear the voice of waters.'

Next, as though a new thought had struck him, he lifted the red axe and kissed the blade.

'Farewell, Inkosi-kaas,' he cried. 'Nay, nay, we will go together; we cannot part, thou and I. We have lived too long one with another, thou and I.

'One more stroke, only one! A good stroke! a straight stroke! a strong stroke!' and, drawing himself to his full height, with a wild heart-shaking shout, he with both hands began to whirl the axe round his head till it looked like a circle of flaming steel. Then, suddenly, with awful force he brought it down straight on to the crown of the mass of sacred stone. A shower of sparks flew up, and such was the almost superhuman strength of the blow, that the massive marble split with a rending sound into a score of pieces, whilst of Inkosi-kaas there remained but some fragments of steel and a fibrous rope of shattered horn that had been the handle. Down with a crash on to the pavement fell the fragments of the holy stone, and down with a crash on to them, still grasping the knob of Inkosi-kaas, fell the brave old Zulu – *dead*.

And thus the hero died.

A gasp of wonder and astonishment rose from all those who witnessed the extraordinary sight, and then somebody cried, '*The prophecy! the prophecy!* He has shattered the sacred stone!' and at once a murmuring arose.

'Ay,' said Nyleptha, with that quick wit which distinguishes her. 'Ay, my people, he has shattered the stone, and behold the prophecy is fulfilled, for a stranger king rules in Zu-Vendis. Incubu, my lord, hath beat Sorais back, and I fear her no more, and to him who hath saved the Crown it shall surely be.'

This spirited speech was met with loud cheering. Then I was supported across the outer courtyard to my old quarters, in order that I might be put to bed.

I was washed and had my mail shirt removed. They hurt me a good deal in getting it off, and no wonder, for my left breast and side was a black bruise the size of a saucer.

The next thing that I remember was the tramp of horsemen outside the palace wall, some ten hours later. I raised myself and asked what was the news, and they told me that a large body of cavalry sent by Curtis to assist the Queen had arrived from the scene of the battle, which they had left two hours after sundown. When they left, the wreck of Sorais' army was in full retreat upon M'Arstuna, followed by all our effective cavalry. Sir Henry was encamping the remains of his worn-out forces on the site (such is the fortune of war) that Sorais had occupied the night before, and proposed marching on to M'Arstuna on the morrow. Having heard this, I felt that I could die with a light heart, and then everything became a blank.

When next I awoke the first thing I saw was the round disc of a sympathetic eye-glass, behind which was Good.

'How are you getting on, old chap?' said a voice from the neighbourhood of the eye-glass.

'What are you doing here?' I asked faintly. 'You ought to be at M'Arstuna – have you run away, or what?'

'M'Arstuna,' he replied cheerfully. 'Ah, M'Arstuna fell last week – you've been unconscious for a fortnight, you see.'

'And Sorais?' I asked.

'Sorais – oh, Sorais is a prisoner; they gave her up, the scoundrels,' he added, with a change of tone – 'sacrificed the Queen to save their skins, you see. She is being brought up here, and I don't know what will happen to her, poor soul!' and he sighed.

'Where is Curtis?' I asked.

'He is with Nyleptha. She rode out to meet us to-day, and there was a grand to-do, I can tell you. He is coming to see you to-morrow; the doctors (for there is a medical "faculty" in Zu-Vendis as elsewhere) thought that he had better not come to-day.'

On the morrow I saw Curtis and Nyleptha with him, and he told me the whole history of what had happened since Umslopogaas and I galloped wildly away from the battle to save the life of the Queen.

As for Nyleptha, she was positively radiant now that 'her dear lord' had come back with no other injury than an ugly scar on his forehead.

'And what art thou going to do with Sorais?' I asked her.

Instantly her bright brow darkened to a frown.

'Sorais,' she said, with a little stamp of the foot; 'ah, but Sorais!'

Sir Henry hastened to turn the subject.

'You will soon be about and all right again now, old fellow,' he said.

I shook my head and laughed.

'Don't deceive yourselves,' I said. 'I may be about for a little, but I shall never be all right again. I am a dying man, Curtis. I may die slow, but die I must. Do you know I have been spitting blood all the morning? I tell you there is something working away into my lung; I can feel it. There, don't look distressed; I have had my day, and am ready to go.'

Here Nyleptha began to cry, and Sir Henry turned the subject, telling me that the artists had taken a cast of the dead body of old Umslopogaas, and that a great statue in black marble was to be erected of him in the act of splitting the sacred stone, which was to be matched by another statue in white marble of myself and the horse Daylight as he appeared when, at the termination of that wild ride, he sank beneath me in the courtyard of the palace.

TWENTY-TWO
I Have Spoken

It was a week after Nyleptha's visit, when I had begun to get about a little in the middle of the day, that a message came to me from Sir Henry to say that Sorais would be brought before them in the Queen's first ante-chamber at midday, and requesting my attendance if possible. Accordingly, greatly drawn by curiosity to see this unhappy woman once more, I made shift, with the help of that kind little fellow Alphonse, who is a perfect treasure to me, and that of another waiting-man, to reach the ante-chamber. I got there, indeed, before anybody else, except a few of the great Court officials who had been bidden to be present, but I had scarcely seated myself before Sorais was brought in by a party of guards, looking as beautiful and defiant as ever, but with a worn expression on her proud face.

A pang of admiration and pity went through me as I looked at her, and struggling to my feet I bowed deeply.

She coloured a little and then laughed bitterly. 'Thou dost forget, Macumazahn,' she said, 'I am no more Queen, save in blood; I am an outcast and a prisoner, one whom all men should scorn, and none show deference to.'

'Thou art a strange woman, Sorais,' I said; 'I pray thee now plead with the Queen Nyleptha, that perchance she may show mercy upon thee.'

She laughed out loud. '*I* plead for mercy!' she said, and at that moment the Queen entered, accompanied by Sir Henry and Good, and took her seat with an impassive face.

'Greeting, Sorais!' said Nyleptha, after a short pause. 'Thou hast rent the kingdom like a rag, thou hast put thousands of my people to the sword, thou hast twice basely plotted to destroy my life by murder, thou has sworn to slay my lord and his companions and to hurl me from the Stairway. What has thou to say why thou shouldst not die?'

'Methinks my sister the Queen hath forgotten the chief count of the indictment,' answered Sorais in her slow musical tones. 'It runs thus: "Thou didst strive to win the love of my lord Incubu." It is for this crime that my sister will slay me, not because I levied war. It is perchance happy for thee, Nyleptha, that I fixed my mind upon his love too late.

'Listen,' she went on, raising her voice. 'I have nought to say save that I would I had won instead of lost. Do thou with me even as thou wilt, O Queen, and let my lord the King there' (pointing to Sir Henry) – 'for now will he be King – carry out the sentence, as it is meet he should, for as he is the beginning of the evil, let him also be the end.' And she drew herself up and shot one angry glance at him.

Sir Henry bent towards Nyleptha and whispered something that I could not catch, and then the Queen spoke.

'Thou shalt not die, Sorais, because my dear lord here hath begged thy life of me as a boon; therefore as a boon and as a marriage gift give I it to him, to do with even as he wills, knowing that, though thou dost love him, he loves thee not, Sorais, for all thy beauty.'

Sorais flushed up to her eyes.

'I thank thee, most gracious Queen and royal sister,' she said, 'for the loving kindness thou hast shown me from my youth up, and especially in that thou hast been pleased to give my person and my fate as a gift to the Lord Incubu – the King that is to be.

'But little can you understand of me, Queen Nyleptha and my Lords, if ye know not that for me there is no middle path; that I scorn your pity and hate you for it; that I cast off your forgiveness as though it were a serpent's sting; and that standing here, betrayed, deserted, insulted, and alone, I yet triumph over you, mock you, and defy you, one and all, and *thus* I answer you.' And then of a sudden, before anybody guessed what she intended to do, she drove the little silver spear she carried in her hand into her side with such a strong and steady aim that the keen point projected through her back, and she fell prone upon the pavement.

Nyleptha shrieked, while the rest of us rushed towards her. But Sorais of the Night lifted herself upon her hand, and for a moment fixed her glorious eyes intently on Curtis's face, as though there were some message in the glance, then dropped her head and sighed, and with a sob her dark but splendid spirit passed.

It was a month after the last act of the Sorais' tragedy that a great ceremony was held in the Flower Temple, and Curtis was formally declared King-Consort of Zu-Vendis. I was too ill to go myself; and, indeed, I hate all that sort of thing, with the crowds and the trumpet-blowing and banner-waving; but Good, who was there (in his full-dress uniform), came back much impressed, and told me that Nyleptha had looked lovely, and Curtis had borne himself in a right royal fashion, and had been received with acclamations that left no doubt as to his popularity.

Afterwards, too, Sir Henry, or rather the King, came to see me, looking very tired, and vowing that he had never been so bored in his life; but I dare say that that was a slight exaggeration.

It was immediately after this ceremony that I caused myself to be moved to the house where I am now writing. That was five months ago, during the whole of which time I have, being confined to a kind of couch, employed my leisure in compiling this history of our wanderings from my journal and our joint memories.

It is a week since I wrote the above, and now I take up my pen for the last time, for I know that the end is at hand. My brain is still clear and I can manage to write, though with difficulty. The pain in my lung, which has been very bad during the last week, has suddenly quite left me, and been succeeded by a feeling of numbness of which I cannot mistake the meaning. And just as the pain has gone, so with it all fear of that end has departed, and I feel only as though I were going to sink into the arms of an unutterable rest.

The sinking sun is turning the golden roof of the great Temple to a fiery flame, and my fingers tire.

So to all who have known me, or know of me, to all who can think one kindly thought of the old hunter, I stretch out my hand from the far-off shore and bid a long farewell.

And now into the hands of Almighty God, who sent it, do I commit my spirit.

'*I have spoken*,' as the Zulus say.

TWENTY-THREE
By Another Hand

A year has elapsed since our most dear friend Allan Quatermain wrote the words '*I have spoken*' at the end of his record of our adventures. Nor should I have ventured to make any additions to the record had it not happened that by a most strange accident a chance has arisen of its being conveyed to England.

The messenger who is to go – and I wish him joy of his journey – is Alphonse. For a long while he has been wearied to death of Zu-Vendis and its inhabitants. He complains dreadfully of the absence of cafés and theatres, and moans continually for his lost Annette, of whom he says he dreams. At any rate, he has determined to brave the horrors of a journey of almost unprecedented difficulty and danger, and also to run the risk of falling into the hands of the French police.

Poor Alphonse! we shall be very sorry to part with him; but I sincerely trust, for his own sake and also for the sake of this history, which is, I think, worth giving to the world, that he may arrive in safety. If he does, and can carry the treasure we have provided him with in the shape of bars of solid gold, he will be, comparatively speaking, a rich man for life, and well able to marry his Annette, if she is still in the land of the living and willing to marry her Alphonse.

Anyhow, on the chance, I may as well add a word or two to dear old Quatermain's narrative.

He died at dawn on the day following that on which he wrote the last words of the last chapter. Nyleptha, Good and myself were present, and a most touching and yet in its way beautiful scene it was. As day broke he asked to be lifted up to watch the rising of the sun for the last time.

'In a very few minutes,' he said, after gazing earnestly at it, 'I shall have passed through those golden gates.'

Ten minutes afterwards he raised himself and looked us fixedly in the face.

'I am going a stranger journey than any we have taken together. Think of me sometimes,' he murmured. 'God bless you all. I shall wait for you.' And with a sigh he fell back.

Good read the Burial Service over him in the presence of Nyleptha and myself, and then his remains were, in defer- ence to the popular clamour, accorded a great public funeral, or rather cremation. I could not help thinking, however, as I marched in that long and splendid procession up to the Temple, how he would have hated the whole thing could he have been there to see it, for he had a horror of ostentation.

And so, a few minutes before sunset, on the third night after his death, they laid him on the brazen flooring before the altar, and waited for the last ray of the setting sun to fall upon his face. Presently it came, and struck him like a golden arrow, crowning the pale brows with glory, and then the trumpets blew, and the flooring revolved, and all that remained of our beloved friend fell into the furnace below.

And so ended the very remarkable and adventurous life of Hunter Quatermain.

Henry Curtis

December 15, 18—